ALSO BY JEREMY BRONAUGH

This Book is Not For Sale and You'd Be a Fool to Buy It: Stories

WHEN YOU BLEED TO DEATH

Jeremy Bronaugh

Hypertrophic Press

WHEN YOU BLEED TO DEATH.
Copyright © 2014 by Jeremy Bronaugh
Previously published as *A Dream Undone*

SECOND EDITION

All rights reserved. No part of this book may be used or reproduced in any manner whatsoever without written permission except in the case of brief quotations embodied in critical articles and reviews.

For information about permission to reproduce selections from this book, write to Hypertrophic Press at P.O. Box 423, New Market, AL, 35761, USA.

This is a work of fiction. Names, characters, places, and incidents are either the product of the author's imagination or are used fictitiously. Any resemblance to actual events, locales, or persons – living or dead – is entirely coincidental.

ISBN-13: 978-0692318942
ISBN-10: 0692318941

Hypertrophic Press
P.O. Box 423, New Market, AL, 35761
www.hypertrophicpress.com

Jeremy Bronaugh can be reached via email @
whenyoubleedtodeath@live.com

for
anyone who's ever sat up until dawn thinking about what it would feel like to be dead

acknowledgments

Lynsey Morandin
Eric Hovis
Grant Niezgodski
Trent Chance
Joshua Bronaugh
Mike Guillebeau
John Molnar
Nichole Saunders, Cheryl Rydbom, Paul Lees-Haley, Judy Rich, Linda Ridenour, Jamie Batson
John Bronaugh
Jerilynn Bronaugh

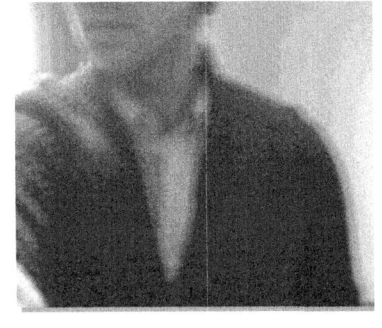

WHEN YOU BLEED TO DEATH

ONE

"Do you know what you're doing, Brody?" James asks.

He tenses his mouth to say something else, but doesn't.

I lean against the porch steps as he slips his hand into his bag and produces a 20-oz. Vanilla Coke bottle that he's filled with Dextromethorphan. DXM. I catch my reflection in the rose lenses of his sunglasses and realize that I haven't given his question much thought.

Before today, I've never done drugs.

"An over-the-counter bottle of Robitussin DM has enough DXM to take an average person to the first plateau." He explains a series of plateaus – levels of consciousness that '60s-era hippies achieved with DXM – each more intense than the last. According to James, DXM users have reported being abducted by aliens and melting into the sun and meeting God. I don't want to cut him off, but I'm not really listening. "This," he stops, choosing his words carefully, "this batch is as strong as it gets."

I reach out and he hands me the bottle.

"You seriously look like shit. When was the last time you ate?"

I haven't eaten since she died. Over a week ago. As I unscrew the cap, a putrid wave of chemical stench washes over me.

"This is the most rancid shit I've ever smelled," I say.

"You really don't have to take it. I'm worried about how you're going to react, you know, with how you feel."

I roll the bottle in my hands and envision James in his mom's kitchen, huddled over the stove in his sunglasses and a "Kiss the Cook" apron, pouring lighter fluid and ammonia into a bubbling pot of cough syrup. He sprinkles glittering pixie dust into the pot. The guaifenesin separates. He ladles it out. The pot simmers. The ammonia evaporates. He wipes the condensation from his glasses, carefully pours his work through a funnel, and – poof – he's sitting on my porch with enough liquid hallucination for me to see my dead girlfriend.

"You didn't answer me," he says. "Do you know what you're doing?"

I think about why I called James; I think about Valerie. Her robin's egg eyes sparkle like springtime, and just as quickly the memory fades.

"We'll see," I say before I choke down the whole bottle, stopping to gag at least twice. Gasoline couldn't taste any worse.

I throw up, but catch it in my mouth and swallow it.

"You've got about forty-five minutes before you're going to feel disconnected," James says. "They call it robo-tripping for a reason." He suddenly remembers to ask, "Are you on any prescription antihistamines?"

I shake my head.

"The drug interaction would make your eyes bleed," he says.

I sigh and taste the lighter fluid in the soda. "Thanks, James," I say and stand up to walk into my house.

"Brody. This wasn't your fault."

I look back at him and nod as I close the door. Through my window I watch James back out of the driveway, watch his shit car disappear, and I pull the shades to drown the morning light.

I notice a dried smear of blood on the sheets as I pull my blanket aside to lie on my bed and wait for her. The awful taste of DXM lingers in my mouth.

An LCD clock glows on my dresser next to a framed picture of Valerie. Her smile lights up her cheeks. I watch as the numbers change, counting the minutes until I'll see her again.

The numbers begin to slowly melt from the clock's display, dripping onto the dresser. I run my hand over the length of my face as I watch. Holding my bottom lip against my chin with my middle finger, I glide the tip of my index finger over a row of teeth I find hidden in my mouth. The longer I spend fingering the bucket of teeth, the more I smell lighter fluid and I don't like the smell, so I stop.

Everything itches.

I stand up and smash the glass in the frame. The sound echoes and I worry that it could wake my mother, who's still sleeping upstairs. I stand motionless, waiting for the sound of creaking floorboards or footsteps.

When I'm satisfied she didn't hear it, I carefully pull the shards of glass from the frame. A piece slips from my hand and cuts my thumb, covering it in slick, greasy blood. My fingers are longer than usual, and I struggle to use them to peel Valerie out of the frame. I stare into the photo and for a second I remember what it had been like to smell her skin.

At Valerie's wake I saw this guy from school, Jason. He was interning at the funeral home over the summer and he was there when the fire department brought her in. I caught him before the wake and asked him to open her coffin.

Jason looked at me for a long time before he said, "She was so messed up when she got here, Brody. It was gruesome." When I didn't say anything, he added, "You don't want to see her like that."

"I need to," I said, and he opened it.

She looked like a mannequin covered in latex skin and an old woman's makeup. I wanted to kiss her, but couldn't bring myself to touch the lifeless body.

I turn her photo over in my hands and see that a small pool of blood has formed in my palm. I set the photo down, accidentally dragging my bloody fingers across her face.

At the burial some stranger told me, "I hear it was a pretty bad wreck. There's no pain when the neck snaps like that." Like he would know.

I slide the glass fragments into my sock drawer, keeping the biggest shard. I close my fist around it until blood leaks through my fingers. I squeeze until the telephone rings, distracting me, and I set the bloody shard next to Valerie.

The ring echoes and I can feel it touch my skin.

I lift the receiver away from my ear and bite hard into my bottom lip as a chorus of voices asks, "How are you holding up?" Other voices tell me how sorry they are. Some of the voices sound familiar. Some of the voices cry.

"Are you there?" the voices ask. "Are you okay?"

They all get the same sobbing word-salad, the same lifeless robotic babble. They say things like "I'm so sorry" and "I'm here for you" and "It will be okay."

Blood trails down my hand and drips onto the mouthpiece of the phone.

I watch myself talking in the mirror. My eyes are swollen. My hair is matted and wild. Water drips from my face and I realize that I'm crying.

I ask the voices what time it is. When they don't

answer, I tell them Broderick isn't available and hang up.

Suddenly the light through the window blinds is excruciating. I open them and see that the world has dissolved into a painful white light.

It pulsates and tells me, "You are alone."

The phone rings again. I cough and lighter fluid rises in my throat, but the phone keeps ringing so I unplug it from the wall.

I have to find her. I did this to find her.

I dive into the ocean of my burgundy comforter and swim deep into the darkness of cream-colored sheets. The bubbles that escape my mouth rise slowly to the top of the ocean and make a familiar sound: Valerie.

My blood clouds the water so I swim deeper, pushing my arms through the resistance, feeling it spread through my fingers.

From the abyss, an ancient predator emerges like a biblical leviathan. The voids of its eyes are set against the colorless bone scales of its face. It could engulf me, tear me into strips of meat against its jagged teeth. I kick wildly, pushing out with frantic strokes. I push as hard as I am able, but it follows at my heels. Exhausted, I gasp for air and water fills my mouth. With a final gasp, I turn and reach out toward the monster.

His hollow eyes follow me as I descend into the void. I sink until his eyes fade.

In the depths of the black and unwelcoming ocean, as with everywhere else lately,

I find nothing.

TWO

I slump over my desk and bury my head in my arms, avoiding the swirl of summer stories from my annoyingly lively classmates.

"Hello and good morning, students," the principal's voice drones over the intercom, "and welcome back for the first day of the school year." I zone out as he rambles through the announcements until he says, "I would like to acknowledge the passing of one of our students. Valerie Robinson. She was involved in a car accident this summer and is no longer with us."

He calls for a moment of silence. The other students bow their heads in feigned mourning. A few rows over, a girl pokes her friend and whispers, then points at me.

Tears well up in my eyes before I make it through the door. In a bathroom stall I grip the toilet rim and vomit. I drop to my knees, gasping for breath, and chuck again. I'm not sure if I'm throwing up from gagging or gagging from throwing up.

I have been in love with Valerie for two years.

Bile leaks from my nose. I throw up again.

I am seventeen years old.

I stay home for the rest of the week.

My father wakes me up on Monday morning and says, "You need to go to school today."

I roll over. "Leave me alone."

"Get up," he repeats, so I do.

I go through the routine of getting dressed, select my clothes without looking at them. I open my sock drawer and see the photo of Valerie, her face stained with dried blood, and I put my shoes on without socks.

"You have an appetite this morning?" Mom asks as she motions to a plate of eggs and toast. I pour a glass of water, and she asks, "Have you been crying?"

"No."

"Sweetie," she says, on the verge of tears. I stand rigid as she hugs me. "You can talk to me about it."

My father drives me to school and waits in the parking lot until I walk into the building. The halls are full of people I should be excited to see, but none of them are her.

One of Valerie's friends, Tiffany, is standing by my locker talking to someone. She waves her friend on when she sees me.

"Hey, Brody," Tiffany says, books held to her chest, covering the low neckline of her shirt. "How are you feeling?"

"Fine." I roll the combination on my locker, opening it out of habit, but nothing is inside.

"You look like shit," she says. "Have you been sleeping at all?"

"I'm fine," I repeat, feeling drained.

She looks into the locker. "You going to get a lot done today with no books or backpack? Want to borrow a pencil at least?"

I take a deep breath as I close the locker and lean my forehead against the door.

"I know you're not okay," she says. "How could you be? You don't have to pretend." She clasps her books in one arm and plants her free hand on my cheek. "I'm going to call you tonight. Check up on you."

"Up high!" This guy Mark comes up from behind Tiffany and holds his hand up for me to high five him. I look from Tiffany to him, lock eyes but say nothing. He drops his hand to my shoulder. "Sorry man."

I brush his hand off and turn to leave.

"I'll call you!" she yells over the hum of voices in the hall while I walk away. I turn to wave at her as Mark puts his arm around her shoulder.

As I turn the corner I see Valerie's face briefly, but then I realize it's someone else.

I sit with my soccer teammates at lunch. Their expressions sour when I set my tray down. They go silent, like if they say the wrong thing I'll simply dissolve, so I slide to the end of the table.

Nolan sets his tray next to mine and grabs my shoulder as he sits down. He doesn't say anything, which I appreciate, so I take a bite out of my rectangle of pizza.

"Does this taste like the color grey and emptiness to you too, or is just me?"

"Nah, man. That's just government food," Nolan says.

I laugh a little, barely a huff, and Nolan half-smiles at me before he starts eating.

He sits with me in silence until lunch ends. I dump my food in the trash on the way out the door and decide to quit the soccer team.

My friend Chris catches me in the hall as I leave the cafeteria. He smiles at me, but it's forced.

Everyone forces a smile around me. Everyone acts like I'm not a burden.

"Any better today?" he asks.

"What's the difference?"

"Brody, I know it's not the same. I know I don't understand how you feel, not really. But it's going to be okay."

"I'm so sick of hearing that," I say.

"It will be though." He shifts awkwardly, slides his thumb into the strap of his backpack.

"Not for her."

His smile fades. "I've got to go to class."

I nod. He leaves. The bell rings.

I lean against the stairs and watch until the hall clears out. I wonder if school was always this lonely, if Valerie distracted me from it.

I leave and walk home.

THREE

"How are you feeling?" my psychiatrist asks. The daytime sun reflects off his framed certifications. Shelves full of leather-bound books stand like totems on either side of his oak desk, but he hasn't added a book to his collection since I started coming here when I was fifteen.

He shifts in his seat and asks me the same question.

"I'm just waiting to die," I say flatly. I sit on a tight leather couch designed for show and not for comfort, the leather too slick, like it's been polished. I resent him because he doesn't have a chaise lounge chair.

"That's normal," he says, crossing his legs. "I'd be worried about you if you said otherwise. When things like this happen, it's the people who don't respond to it that are in the most danger."

A week ago I took all of the pills in my parents' medicine cabinet – every white chalky heart pill, every slick purple and shiny yellow capsule. When people use pills to kill themselves in a movie it's always hurried, a snap decision, and then they fade off with a serene look like they're dreaming; it took me twenty minutes and two bottles of water to even get the pills down.

"It's normal to wish you were dead?"

"I wouldn't worry about it," he says. Scribbles on a legal pad.

For several hours I writhed naked on my bathroom floor in agony. My stomach wrenched and churned in my throat. My heart beat black grease through my veins. Every minute that passed, I wished harder for death. I threw up on the floor and would have cleaned it up, but instead I lay naked in the vomit until morning.

"You're grieving," he says. "It isn't going to be easy. Are you still self-harming?"

"I don't want to talk about that."

"Okay," he says, "what do you want to talk about?"

"Can't you just prescribe something?" I say. "I don't want to feel like this anymore."

He shakes his head. "You're a prime candidate for substance abuse, Brody. We've talked about this."

I leave his office and his secretary makes an appointment for me that I have no intention of keeping. When I get in my car I sit in the parking lot for a long time and cry.

A counselor pulls me from third block when I get back to school after my psychiatric appointment. In her office she tells me that skipping school is a disruptive behavior that she won't tolerate. I show her the note from the shrink.

"That's not good enough," she says from behind her cheap metal desk. "We all know how upset you are, but we can't have you disrupting the other students, can we?"

"How does me not going to class disrupt the students who are in class?" I ask.

She assigns me to alternative school for the rest of the day, isolating me from the rest of the student body, forgetting how important my presence is to class.

I fold the a-school slip into my coat pocket and walk to my car in the parking lot. I drive downtown and leave my car in a garage while I take a walk across the Second Street bridge.

I stop halfway, standing over the Ohio River between Kentucky and Indiana. I wonder how many people jump, how long it would take for my body to wash up.

Mom is waiting for me at the front door when I get home. Apparently the counselor tipped her off when she saw me leave. Mom takes me to get ice cream.

"I don't want anything," I say when we get there.

Mom orders two vanilla milkshakes.

We sit across from each other in a booth. Neither of us says anything, but I drink the milkshake.

FOUR

I skip fourth block. After the bell rings, I find Chris's class and ask his teacher if I can talk to him. She looks at him, then to me, and says, "Go ahead."

"What's up, Brody?" he asks in the hallway.

"I don't know," I say. "I just don't see the point in being here anymore."

"At school?"

"Sure," I say. I lean on the wall and slide to the floor.

"You know," Chris says, "everything happens for a reason."

"I didn't come for therapy," I say.

"You have to talk about it eventually, Brody. It's been weeks."

"Fine. So what validates her dying? Rationalize it."

"I don't know," he says, "but there has to be a reason."

Fate. This is the easiest way for anyone to write off that she's dead and move on.

"Let's say it wasn't random," I say, thinking about the day she died. "If a butterfly didn't just flap its wings and fuck up my life, then I caused this."

"No you didn't. It was an accident. You weren't even in the car," he says.

"It can't happen for a reason and be an accident.

Saying it has some purpose doesn't make it okay. That's like saying it'd make sense to me if I already understood it."

"Well, what do you want me to say? One of my best friends died for no reason and now I'm watching the other one kill himself for nothing. For no reason at all."

"I already told you I don't want you to say anything."

Chris gives me a ride after school. I light a cigarette as we pull out of the parking lot.

"Hey, don't smoke in my car. When did you even start smoking?"

I flick the cigarette out the window. "About a week ago."

Chris frowns. He knew Valerie his whole life, even introduced me to her, but I can't bring myself to ask him how he feels about her dying. He stops for gas, and I get out of the car and lean against it while I light another cigarette.

"So, the guy who theorized infinity died in a mental institution," Chris says as he lifts the gas pump from its station.

"Why?" I ask.

"Like, how did he die or why was he put there?"

"Both."

"Oh." He scratches his head like he hadn't considered it. "I don't know."

This shithead, Saul, pulls up at the pump across from us. My father works with Saul's. As a child my parents would drop me off at his house and I would endure his best attempts to harass me. Years into our mock friendship he slammed my head into the cleave of a wall, splitting the skin above my eye. To this day a scar runs through my left eyebrow.

My parents stopped making me go to his house

after that.

The pump releases and I look back across the car at Chris. He notices Saul, then my pensive expression. "I'm gonna pay. Just don't even talk to that piece of crap. I'll be right back. And put that cigarette out before you blow us up."

I grind the tip of the cigarette between my fingers as Chris walks off into the gas station.

"Brody!" Saul yells as he gets out of his car. "How are you lately? I heard you ain't doing so hot." There's a kind of hollowness to his voice that I never noticed before.

"Fuck off, Saul."

"I heard this rumor," he says, walking toward me, "that your lady killed herself 'cause you broke up with her."

Before she died, Valerie made a point to talk to all of her old friends, even people she hadn't talked to in years. She called her teachers from grade school, an old babysitter, wrote letters to people she couldn't reach.

He couldn't possibly know that she talked about suicide every day. The only person I mentioned it to was James.

"Who said that?" I ask, half choking.

"Doesn't matter. What matters is you haven't denied it."

"It was a wreck, you fuck. Who said that?"

His cheeks rise, drawing back into a smile so fake and calculated he looks like a jack-o-lantern. I'm eight years old again, and watching me suffer is a game. He shifts his posture and starts to say something, so I slam my fist into his jaw, knocking him into Chris's car.

"Who the fuck said that!?" I scream.

He catches himself and stumbles toward me. "Fuck you, you little bitch." He tries to stand up straight so I slam his head into Chris's passenger-side window. It cracks, a spider web forming instantly in the glass.

"Who the fuck said that!?"

He hawks and spits on me.

I cock back to hit Saul again, but someone grabs my shoulders so I throw my other elbow back wildly. I feel it connect.

Chris stumbles back and sputters, "God! What the hell!?"

Seeing Chris doubled over, both hands covering his face, I realize what I've done.

A small crowd has gathered around us. Saul kneels against the concrete. He looks up at me and says, "I'm going to fucking kill you."

"We need to get out of here, like now," Chris chokes out as he scrambles to the other side of the car, starts it, and pulls forward. He idles, waiting for me.

"You're fucking dead, Brody. You can fucking join her." Saul struggles to stand up, loses his balance.

As I get in the car I hear someone in the crowd say, "What a psycho."

Chris speeds away, nose still bleeding. "What the hell got into you?"

"I don't know," I tell him. And I don't. My hands shake. I clench and unclench my fists to try and steady them. I think about the voice in the crowd. *What a psycho.* Then I light a cigarette, and some of Saul's blood stains the filter.

FIVE

"He asked me to marry him. Can you believe that?" Tiffany chimes in my ear on what has become her nightly phone call. What started as a chore, her calling to check up on me, has become the high point of my day.

"Mark?"

"No. I wish. Chad."

"The crazy one?" I ask as I settle into bed.

"Yes!" she says excitedly. "He just showed up at my window in the middle of the night and asked me to marry him."

"Am I invited to the wedding?"

She scoffs. "And the ring cost him two hundred dollars. Can you believe that? What kind of girl would say yes to such a cheap ring? He threatened to kill himself, too, when I said no."

"Did he kill himself right there or leave to do it?"

She laughs again.

"How many boyfriends do you have at any given time?"

"I'd give them all up for you."

"I'm never going to date again," I say.

"Women all over the world are mourning thanks to that."

"Valerie's dad rerecorded his answering machine message," I say quickly, moving away from her come on. "I'll never hear her voice again."

"Oh, Brody," she sighs, "I'm so sorry. I miss her too."

"I lose more of her every day," I say, feeling guilty for bringing it up at all.

The call waiting tone sounds in my phone. "Hold on," I say and switch lines. "Hello?"

"I'll be there in ten minutes," James says curtly.

"Cool." He hangs up, and I click over to Tiffany. "I've got to go."

"What are you doing?" she asks.

"Nothing," I say. "I just have to go."

"Okay. Have fun," she says as I hang up.

I throw my shoes on and grab my wallet before climbing out of my window, following the shadows away from my house and then up the street to wait at the mouth of my neighborhood. James stops in the middle of the road and leans over to open the door for me. I climb in and light a joint.

"Take these," James says as he fishes in his pocket for a small pill bottle: STACKERS. Before I even ask, he offers, "Ephedrine is a stimulant truckers use to stay awake on long trips. It's in the amphetamine family." We pull into a ragged-looking neighborhood. "The high from those will help you balance the down from the pot."

I pour myself a handful and swallow them with spit.

"Don't take too many or you'll get pulmonary edema."

He pulls into a neighborhood and parks in the driveway of a house with a FOR SALE sign in its yard. We let ourselves in through the back door. Two freshman girls look up at me vacantly from their seat on the floor. This older-looking surfer-jock next to them, easily twenty-five, strums an acoustic guitar, but I can't hear the chords over the rock music playing on a portable radio next to him.

I wonder if pulmonary edema would kill me, whatever the fuck it is.

"I've got someone I want you to meet," James says as I follow him upstairs into another room with no furniture. "Brody, meet Puck." He points to a forty-year-old man sitting in a circle of high-schoolers. Puck takes a puff off a ceramic pipe and then hands it to a boy about my age before he stands up, brushes his overalls off, and ambles over to me.

"This the guy?" Puck asks. James nods. Puck extends his hand and I shake it before realizing how clammy I am. I pull the collar of my hoodie away from my chest, noticing that my undershirt is soaked through with sweat. "Nice to meet you, man," Puck says. "So what are you looking for?"

I look to James. Puck tucks back a smile and continues. "Don't worry, man. Whatever you need, I got it."

SIX

I wake up drenched in sweat. After peeling the pillow from my face, I rotate my neck slowly while registering how hard it is to sit up. The alarm clock on my dresser next to the broken frame flashes like the power went out.

I walk upstairs through the unlit house to see what time it is and realize it's already five. I slept through school.

"Hello?" I yell to no answer.

I open my father's liquor cabinet and pour a glass of bourbon. Back in my room, I use it to chase three hydrocodone pills from the baggie Puck sold me.

There are two boxes under my bed; one full of photographs, the other X-Acto knives. I pull out the photo box and sit on my bed. In the first photo Valerie leans her head into my chest, her smile so bright I can see it in her eyes. Her mom snapped the picture before the winter formal last year.

I tear it in half, ripping through my matching shirt and tie, and then into my face. Then I rip up the halves, mutilating her once beautiful blue eyes.

I shred through all of the photographs: first the roll from the formal and then some from random dates before I go through her school portraits. Then a picture of her and her little sister.

Tears roll down my face as I destroy the last photograph, an old-time mock-up that Valerie's mother forced her to take a month before she died. She holds a silk rose against her chin with a look of disdain. Her eyes look lost and emotionless.

They look dead.

I sweep the remnants into the trash and use my shirt to wipe my face. My parents' car pulls into the driveway so I lock my door and turn off the light. I listen as they walk into the house, expecting them to come downstairs to check on me. When they don't, I take three more pills and down what's left of my drink.

The phone rings.

"I missed you at school," Tiffany says.

"Yeah," I say weakly.

She must hear me crying because her tone changes. "Do you like beds?" she asks.

"Who doesn't?" I set the empty photo box on the floor and lie down.

"I'm lying in one now," she says. "What about blankets?"

"They're okay."

"Brody," she says.

"Tiffany," I answer.

"We have so much in common." She sighs heavily before adding, "Stay on the phone with me until I fall asleep."

I'm not sure which one of us falls asleep first.

SEVEN

This girl, Cheryl, sits across from me in third period painting a blocky flower on a square piece of wood. "Bathroom art," she calls it. She finished three of them yesterday.

I stare at my own blank piece of canvas board.

"I think people should look at themselves in the mirror naked at least an hour a day," Cheryl says from behind her painting.

I nod, then look up at her and realize she can't see me, so I say, "Sure." She brushes her black hair away from her eyes, smearing paint against her cheek.

I drag my thumb over the grainy canvas and my eyes fall on the thin white scar I earned removing Valerie's photograph from its frame over a month ago. I rub my forefinger against the scar while I stare at my canvas.

It looks just like the gauze I use after I cut.

I fish in my pocket for my Swiss Army Knife. Two other students are painting at another table, and Mrs. Gardner is leafing through a jewelry catalogue at her desk.

Under the table, I open the knife and maneuver it under my shirt sleeve. I feel my skin tear and close my eyes. Taking a deep breath, I press the tip of the blade into the cut and drag it along my forearm.

"I just think, like, that people should learn to love

themselves," Cheryl says. She stops painting to look across the table at me. I smile at her and say I agree as I force the knife deeper into my arm.

"You get me, Brody." She smiles at me sincerely before focusing on painting again.

I blot a paper towel against the cut, waiting for it to absorb, and then drag it against the canvas, smearing the blood into the grain.

I mix paint to match it and cover the entire board in simulated blood.

A small spot has bled into my shirt, but it's nothing anyone would notice.

The next day I scrutinize my painting as Cheryl works on hers. "What do you think of adding words to these?" she asks, holding up her newest piece. "Like 'hope,' 'joy,' you know – stuff like that."

"Too much," I say. "You're supposed to *feel* art, right?"

"Sure, but I want to add a message." She puckers her lips like she's waiting for me to shoot her motivational woodblocks down.

"Do you think it would matter?"

"It couldn't hurt," she says and dips a new brush in white paint, adding 'HOPE' to the bottom of one of her paintings. As she does this I look back at mine and decide to add 'EVERY DAY IS THE WORST DAY OF MY LIFE' along its base. I set it up to dry and immediately start another one, covering the painting in faux blood. Then, over the blood, I paint a revolver and write 'TODAY I POLISH MY REVOLVER FOR THE LAST TIME.'

"I really love these," Cheryl says before class ends. I tell her that I like hers too and go to fourth period.

On Friday I start a third in the series. I repeat the bloody base, but can't think of anything to add to it, so I light a cigarette. I take a few drags before Mrs. Gardner walks over from her desk and says, "Seriously, Brody? Put that out."

I grind the cigarette into the canvas.

"Is this what you're working on?" she says, studying my painting. I nod and lay the first two on the table in sequence. "These are amazing," she says. "Can I display them in the lobby?"

An hour later she pulls me out of English class.

"I'm so sorry," she says, "but the principal took your paintings down." She puts her hand on my shoulder. Her expression wavers briefly. "He destroyed them. I would have stopped him, but he did it before I even knew."

"That's okay," I say.

"I'm as mad about it as you can imagine."

"No, really." I smile to reassure her. "It's okay."

EIGHT

Slivers of moonlight hitch rides on passing cars as James and I drive into Louisville's slums.

"You'll like Beth," James promises as he whips into a trailer park, skidding on the gravel road. He parks and I follow him past several identical trailers until we get to the one without stairs to its elevated door. He huddles awkwardly on a wooden step stool as he knocks. Inside, someone stomps around slamming cabinets. The door is so thin it hardly muffles a woman shouting.

I cover my mouth with my hands, breathing heavy to warm them. James turns to me from the stool. "She's cool," he says as he pulls a cigarette from his pocket and lights it.

"Does she know we're coming?" I tuck my hands in my pockets and take a deep breath of autumn air.

A hard-lived woman, maybe fifty, answers the door. She recognizes James and, with a gesture, invites us into what a shipping crate would look like if you filled it with trash and old food. The acrid smell of stale pot is overpowering.

"Who's this?" she questions James.

"Brody," James says.

She stares at James, then me.

"'The best way to find out if you can trust somebody is to trust them,'" I say. "Hemingway."

She glares at me hard, like I'm a moron, then turns her gaze to James. For a second, anything could happen.

"He's cool," James assures her.

She nods and walks into a section of the room that's supposed to serve as a kitchen. I sit on a threadbare couch; the flowers on the print have withered. James sits on an overturned bucket. She returns from the kitchen with an odd plastic vase.

"What is that?" I ask.

She stares at me in bewilderment.

"It's a bong," James says.

"Cool. Where's Beth?" I ask, realizing the woman is probably her mother.

"I'm Beth," she says, and I see her in the light for the first time, really looking at her. I don't know if I'm put out or feel sorry for her, but I don't want to be in her trailer, noticing all the holes in the ceiling or the scars on her face.

I glare at James, who ignores me. Beth packs some pot into a side chamber of the bong and lights it. She sucks a mouthful of smoke before passing it to James, who demonstrates how to take a hit before passing it to me.

"He's learning," James says to Beth. He leans forward on his bucket, shoulders slouched.

I light the bong and take a hit. After a short coughing fit, I hand it off and light a cigarette.

A door creaks in the hallway and a five-year-old girl emerges from a back room. She walks over to Beth and attempts to hug her arm, smiling through a cleft palate and crossed eyes.

"Get back in your room!" Beth snaps. "God. I can't get a fucking minute." She looks at me for sympathy and I'm suddenly very jealous of James, that his glasses hide any expression. She shuffles the girl back into her dungeon and I sink farther into the dying garden of a couch.

We pass the bong around for what feels like an hour. I don't say anything because I'm afraid to sour the situation further. I just lean into the couch and take greedy hits to get as high as possible. When the weed is cashed, James thanks her for having us and we make our way back into the night.

"I feel slimy," I grumble, zipping my track jacket to the collar.

"Take some Stackers," James says as we climb into his car. He gets back on the highway and starts toward the boonies, out of Louisville completely.

"I mean, I know..."

"What?" he asks sharply.

"Fuck it."

Endless rows of trees replace the city's streetlights. James takes a winding back road, twisting sharply along its curves. We ride in the darkness, only lit by the car's headlights until James sees an abandoned, small-town grocery store. He pulls in and puts his high beams on.

"What are we even doing?"

"Just keep the car running," he says as he gets out. He walks to the unlit door and stands beside it. I stamp my cigarette into his seat as a toothless husk of a man emerges from the shop. In the car's headlights the man's skin looks like yellow leather.

They shake hands. The man disappears into the store and James walks back to the car.

"What was that about?" I ask as we pull away.

He lights a cigarette, his face momentarily lit by the flame, and says "Don't worry about it" before stomping on the gas pedal. The car picks up speed, feels less and less connected to anything with each second. I feel loose, like I'm unbelted on a roller coaster.

I lean to see the speedometer: 80 miles an hour.

"You need to slow down, man," I say. "You can't drive like this fucked up."

"I'm a better driver when I'm high." A car passes, its headlights bouncing off James's glasses.

He speeds through another curve, bouncing over humps in the road. He clears another bend and his lights fall on a suicidal deer planted in the middle of the road.

James pulls the steering wheel tight. Overcorrects.

The car skids off the road in slow motion, giving me enough time to realize that I'll probably die. I close my eyes. Breathe in.

The tires leave the road, and the car is suspended in air just long enough for me to acknowledge it before gravity's jealous reaction, its clumsy grasp smashing us into the dirt. I slam shoulder first into the passenger door.

I pause, waiting to be dead.

When I'm not, I open my eyes and exhale. The passenger side of the car is lodged in a ditch against an embankment of dirt. I push against my door. It won't budge, so I lean back and kick it as hard as I can. James has those stupid fucking sunglasses on, watching me kick the door, so I keep kicking it until my leg hurts. He pushes his door open, balancing it precariously on its hinges as he climbs out, then offers me his hand and helps me climb out of the shit heap. He closes the door and we sit on the now skyward facing side of the car, our legs dangling against the undercarriage. The deer looks at us briefly, then bolts into the trees.

"That was awesome," James hisses.

"Fuck you, man."

"You should appreciate it, at least."

"I just feel cheated," I say.

We sit in silence, the ambient sounds of the forest

leaking into the street to fill the lapse in conversation.

"James," I say, "I've been thinking about something a lot and I need an answer from you."

He turns, his glasses catching the moonlight.

"Did you tell Saul what I said about Valerie?" I turn away from him after I ask. I can't see his reaction, so I'm not going to let him see mine.

"What are you talking about?"

All I hear in his answer is that he didn't say no. I tighten my grip against the car, forcing the metal into the flesh of my fingers, hoping they'll bleed.

"You know, Brody," he says, "you've been a real buzzkill all night."

NINE

My father knocks on my door to wake me up.

"Come eat lunch," he says as he steps into my room.

"I'm not hungry," I say, rolling over.

He picks up the broken frame on my dresser and scrutinizes it as he says, "Your mother made lunch." He sets it back in its place and adds "I'm not going to ask again" on his way out the door.

I hear his heavy steps on the stairs and force myself to roll out of bed. I stand up too quickly and want to puke. Feeling dizzy and nauseated, I lean over my dresser, set my forehead on the wood, and feel how cool it is against my skin.

Upstairs, my parents stomp around and clang dishes. I take a deep breath and push off the dresser. I pick a sweatshirt up off my floor and pull it over my head as I trudge up the stairs.

"Set the table, sweetie," my mother says, standing over the stove with a cigarette in her mouth. I pour a glass of water and down it, then gather the dishes and set the table. My father walks into the kitchen and takes his coffee out of the microwave.

"Want some coffee, son?" he asks.

"No," I say, sitting down to wait for them.

Mom brings in the food and dad sits at the other end of the table. We eat in silence until the phone rings and mom hurries out of the room to answer it, leaving me and my father together at the table.

He brings his coffee cup to his lips, speaking over its rising steam. "I know a hangover when I see one, son."

I stop picking at my salad to look at him.

"I know you're having a rough time, but you're only a few months from graduation and then you move on with your life. After you get out of high school you can drink all you want."

"Move on?" I grumble.

"Don't twist my words. I've given you a lot of leeway, but you have to get your act together."

I sit, silently seething, looking at the wall as he talks. When he finishes, I stand up and grab my dishes.

"I didn't excuse you," he says curtly, the tone of his voice shifting from stern to angry.

"I'm going downstairs." Tension spreads through my back as I clench my teeth.

"Sit down," he says. "And don't you dare look at me that way."

"Don't act like you give a fuck about what's happening to me!" I yell.

He jumps up and pushes his chair back in one motion. I slam my dishes on the table and storm out of the room.

"Sweetie?" my mother says, passing me on my way down the stairs. She turns and yells "What'd you say to him now?" at my father.

I slam myself in my room and lock the door.

When I bought the set of X-Acto knives that I keep under my bed, I also bought a model tank just to avoid any questions. The cashier rang up the tank and dropped it in a bag. Then she picked up the knives, turned them over in her hand and scrutinized them; she must have known. And then she asked, "Do you already have the paint? We sell glue and stuff for models on aisle six."

"I've got paint," I lied. "Thank you." I dumped the tank in the trash as soon as I was out the door.

I grab a thin blade and set the box on my bed. I drop my pants, revealing row after row of jagged, overlapping scars. I used to feel so ashamed about cutting myself.

Now I just enjoy it.

The first cut splits the skin. It doesn't even bleed at first.

I'm careful not to make it any wider than my bandages so I won't bleed through my pants again. I put the tip of the blade in the open wound and drag it along the thin, red line, splitting it further. I slice deeper into the cut over and over, each time feeling the intensity of the pain increase.

Blood trickles from the wound at first and then trails down my thigh.

I cut again, letting myself cry as I tear into my muscle. The embers inside me cool and I wipe the blood off of my leg and quickly slap on a large, rectangular bandage. Blood flowers through it immediately, turning the white bandage a deep red.

I put my pants back on and sit on my bed. The veins in my arm, pronounced from clenching for so long, look thin and weak. I drag my bloody finger along them, marking the path I'd need to slice to kill myself.

I press the flat edge of the blade against my vein.

I could cut through them so easily.

There are so many ways to kill myself every day. Every car, bridge, or tall building is a way out, and, with the blade of my favorite knife pressed against my veins, I have to wonder why it was so easy for her.

TEN

I'm sitting on my bed running my fingertip over my pocket knife blade when James calls and asks, "Wanna get high?"

I close the knife. James hasn't said anything to me since the accident, and, although I'm still mad, I really do want to get high.

"I sure do."

I get dressed and wait on my steps for him to show. Trick-or-treaters prowl my neighborhood dressed as ninjas and monsters and princesses. A little boy dressed as Superman sees me sitting on the porch and drags his mother through my yard to yell, "Trick or treat!" He expectantly raises his garbage bag full of candy.

"Trick," I say.

He looks at his mother, confused. She scowls at me and tugs on his arm to drag him to the next house. James pulls up as they walk away. I light a cigarette as I get in his car.

I've never liked Superman.

James passes me a lit joint. His lip twitches, and he looks away.

"What's the plan?" I ask between puffs.

"College thing at U of L," he says. I hold the joint out to pass it back to him, but he waves it away. I finish it as he drives past Cardinal Stadium and pulls into a cramped little neighborhood. We park on the street. He reaches into his backseat and hands me a half-filled Coke bottle.

I twist the lid and smell it: DXM.

"Happy Halloween," he says. I snuff out the joint and wait for him to get out of the car. "Something wrong?" he asks.

I shrug.

"You should drink that before we go in. I only made enough for you."

Behind his opaque glasses I can't tell if he's apologizing or didn't have enough cough syrup for more than one bottle. I smell the lighter fluid. He sits, watching me, so I stomach the smell and take a deep gulp from the bottle. It makes me want to wretch, so I tip the bottle and down the disgusting syrup to get it over with.

We walk into a small house without knocking. Three guys sit on the couch watching music videos and drinking light beer. One of the guys, thin and jagged, is perched on an arm of the couch like a gargoyle. The other two – both dressed in football jerseys – don't bother to look my way.

No one says anything to us.

"Want a drink?" James asks, helping himself to two cans of beer from a cooler by the couch.

I shake my head. "I'll be good in forty-five minutes, right?"

"We'll see," he says and walks off.

I crouch against the wall and light a cigarette, holding the smoke in my mouth to kill the lighter fluid taste. The guy perched on the arm of the couch eyeballs me, but averts his gaze when I catch it. I stare at him outright, letting a plume of smoke roll out of my mouth.

He sees me staring and his gaze lingers. Then he stands up in one motion and walks out of the room.

When he passes in front of the kitchen light it rolls around his body, warping into a physical presence.

Shit.

I check my watch; it's been twenty minutes. I stand up in waves.

This is too soon.

"Remember that I told you to wait," James says to someone off-screen as he emerges in frame. Someone follows behind him, a silhouette eclipsing the kitchen light.

The two guys stand up from the couch and walk toward me. Then the silhouette ripples into focus: Saul.

I take a deep breath. One of the guys steps to my right and punches me in the chest, knuckles into my ribs. The other clamps onto my arm. I yank away from him, but they grab me and pin me to the wall.

"James," I say, looking into those stupid fucking sunglasses.

"Shut up, faggot," Saul says before slamming his fat fist into my jaw. "Fucking faggot pretty boy."

"James," I say, fighting for each syllable.

The gargoyle walks back into the room, shadow obscuring his face. Saul throws a right cross; his knuckles catch in my eye socket. The room lights up, each figure glazed in slick, flickering light.

"James," I say again, struggling to get it out. I pull against the golems on my side, but I'm under water. Saul punches me in the stomach. I heave, the smell of lighter fluid rising in my throat, into my nostrils, and vomit.

"What?" he asks. His red lenses catch the light as he turns his head toward me.

"You're a motherfucker." I strain to enunciate each word.

"Shut your faggot mouth," Saul says, and hits me square in the throat.

ELEVEN

The world breaks down to a collection of forces when you're drugged out of your head. Of whispers bouncing off the metal sound of an engine revving. Of momentum and tight turns and lights that blur into one long, physical bulb stretching down the street.

Everything pulls in a different direction and all I can feel are the hands dragging me out of the car.

Blood builds up in my mouth as I lie on the wet pavement. I try to stand up as the car speeds away, and have to fight the nausea just to bring myself to my knees. Cars blur past like neon streams. Lights above me burn like dying suns and suddenly it's raining.

I don't recognize anything, so I start to panic and force myself to stand up straight. A bright yellow sign glows too bright across the street. The words are blurred, but it's recognizable enough as a diner, so I take a deep breath and step forward. Each step is labored. I focus on holding myself up straight, my arms outstretched for balance.

"Oh my God. Are you okay?" a woman asks. Light rolls off her face in waves.

"I don't. I. I don't."

"Honey, sit down." She's beside me, and in front of me.

"Just. I," I breathe deep. I have to get out of here.

Have to pull myself together long enough to fix this. "Phone," I cough out.

"Of course, sweetie." The lights are so bright I can feel them, and she is handing me the phone and asking what the number is, but I don't know. I take the phone and dial by muscle memory. The ringing reverberates.

"Hello?" Tiffany.

"I need."

"Brody?"

"Help."

"Brody, what are you talking about? Help with what? It's so late."

"Help." I pull it together as much as I can to hand the phone to the woman. "What time is the address?" I ask her.

She takes the phone from me and starts talking, residual echoes of conversations bubbling beside me.

Then she is walking me outside, where I vomit, and she is saying something to me, but the smell of lighter fluid is so overpowering that I can't hear anything, and then the headlights and Tiffany's voice and I'm okay.

"Oh my God," Tiffany says. Her face is so close to mine. Her arms around my neck. "Come on," she says, "get in the car."

Ocean waves carry me away from shore. Faceless people swim around me, throwing beach balls, laughing. Valerie splashes diamond-clear water at me and giggles. I splash her back as I paddle my feet to stay afloat as the waves carry me farther away from her.

She smiles and mouths something to me that I can't understand.

The water around me clouds with black smoke. I look down in time to see the leviathan's eyes emerge from the darkness. It's smaller than I remember, but its hollow, soulless eyes are paralyzing.

I panic, kicking wildly toward Valerie. Her face goes blank and her eyes retract into the same lifeless voids as the monster's. She smiles, revealing a mouth full of jagged, bloody teeth.

I feel the monster's mouth snap shut on my foot like a bear trap. Thrashing and screaming, I beat my free foot against its unflinching face. The water clouds with blood.

I jolt.

Sweat drips from my face as I catch my breath.

"Oh fuck. I'm glad you're awake." Tiffany rubs my chest. "I've been sitting here freaking out about whether or not I should call a hospital."

I focus my eyes on her as she reaches out to me. My mouth tastes like blood. With the shadows cast over her face, I can't see her eyes, only the way her mouth moves as she asks, "What happened to you?"

TWELVE

I wake to a large, beige bedroom covered in band posters. My ribs ache as I sit up, then I make the mistake of breathing in and groan. Tiffany pops through the door.

"Oh, thank God," she says. "I was so worried about you." She touches my temple. "I wanted to take you to the hospital, but you were so high. I just didn't know what to do."

I stand up slowly, experimentally, remembering how hard it was last time.

"You really scared the shit out of me."

"I'm sorry." I can't handle the worried look on her face – I'm embarrassed to have involved her at all – so I look around the room to avoid eye contact.

"It's almost two," she says. "Do you want something to eat?"

"No," I say. "Let me just call a cab and I'll get out of your way."

"You're not in my way. You can take a shower here. Get the blood off your face. But I don't have any clothes that will fit you," she says, pointing to the black, bloody spit-stain on my shirt.

"It's okay," I say. "Where's your phone?"

"I'm not sending you home like that," she says, pointing toward her bathroom. "Get cleaned up."

I shower, then inspect myself in her mirror. My

face is covered in shiny black welts and I feel a knot swelling on my temple. I grab my nose and wiggle it from side to side; it hurts, but it isn't broken. I tongue the split in my lip and then poke at the swelling around my blackened eyes.

I find some rubbing alcohol and cotton swabs in her medicine cabinet and I clean the cuts on my face. I fill her trashcan with bloodstained, black cotton before I use my finger to brush my teeth.

Dressed in my bloody clothes, I walk back into her room and ask, "Will you please give me a ride home?"

"Brody, isn't your mom home during the day? You can't go home looking like that."

"I don't have much choice." I sigh. "Even if I change my clothes, she's going to see my face."

"We can minimize it at least. I can use some concealer to cover the bruises." Her voice is filled with an unfamiliar empathy.

"There's no point. You can't do that every day. I can't hide it."

"At least let me get you out of those gross clothes." Her voice waivers. "Even if you don't think it matters, your mom doesn't deserve to see you like that."

I want to refuse her, but she's right.

We drive to the mall where I trudge through the crowd, fighting the toxic buildup in my muscles. In this metro store she likes, she scrutinizes a rainbow of polo shirts, selecting one in seafoam green to hold against my skin.

"That'll look nice," she says. "It really compliments the purple bruises all over your face."

"Hilarious," I say, taking the shirt. I don't own a shirt on the light side of the color spectrum, but I just smile and let her charge it.

I change in the dressing room. When I pull my bloody shirt over my head, I can't ignore the spectrum of bruises. The old, sepia ones from the car accident bleed into the new, purple ones all over my chest and arms. The blackened smears around my kidney ooze down as if they were viscous, barely connecting to the fresh cuts sneaking from my thigh onto my waistline. I huff and pull on the seafoam shirt.

"You have to eat something," Tiffany says as we drive downtown, "even if you aren't hungry. Just eat a little bit."

I lean back in my seat. Tiff stops at a light and I read a billboard with a public service announcement about how to spot a meth addict.

"If you insist," I say.

We park on the street downtown and sit outside at a little café. It's the first day of November, but the afternoon warms us enough that I can relax against the metal chair. The waiter is kind enough not to mention my face, and the food is good.

"Do you want to get coffee?" I ask Tiffany after we eat.

"I thought you didn't like coffee," she says.

"I don't," I say. "I just wanted to sit with you a little longer."

THIRTEEN

James is slinking through the parking lot when I pull into school on Monday morning. I watch him disappear into the side entrance as I rub my palm over my swollen face.

I wanted to stay in this morning, but it wasn't worth Mom seeing me like this. She caught me on my way out the door anyway, just to tell me to have a good day, and bawled uncontrollably.

James.

I suck a final draw off my cigarette, flick it into the grass, and follow him into school. I brush past some girl and grab James's collar before I slam his head into a locker so hard it dents the door.

He swings at me, but he's disoriented, so I catch his arm and slam his head into the locker again.

Other students, smelling blood, swarm us and form a circle.

"You were my fucking friend!" I yell as I stomp on his chest.

I'm about to stomp again when he stammers, "Wait. Wait. What are you talking about?"

"What the fuck do you think I'm talking about?" I scream though gritted teeth.

"Oh, yeah." He takes off his sunglasses, folding them carefully. I'm so used to seeing him in sunglasses that I didn't even know his eyes were blue.

"About that: you're always talking about how much you want to die. I didn't really think you would have a problem with it," he says, his voice low and haunting.

His answer makes a lot more sense than I wanted it to.

The bell rings as a vice principal jumps between me and James. He yells for the crowd to clear out.

"What happened here?" he asks James.

"I fell," James says.

The principal looks from me to James and back and says to both of us, "Act like men and handle your shit outside of school."

FOURTEEN

"I've missed you," Tiffany says as we pass a joint back and forth in my car before going to the Homecoming football game. "You're lucky that guy didn't press charges, though."

"He wouldn't want the attention," I say.

"When are you allowed back at school?"

"Another week. I'm not even supposed to be here."

"As much school as you miss I'm surprised they think suspension is a punishment." She passes the joint back to me, nearly cashed. I take a puff and throw the roach in the parking lot.

"Why don't you save those?" she asks.

"Why bother?" I don't mention that I hate pot – the smell, the taste, the haze it puts me in. Every time I smoke pot I feel slow for two days.

I buy tickets and we walk toward the bleachers. The game is in full swing. A football soars through the air and people stand up and scream. Tiff breaks away from me and approaches a group of girls. They hug. Laugh.

I turn away and walk to the concession stand where I buy two trays of nachos with extra cheese, two hot dogs loaded with relish, two small cheeseburgers, a package of Reese's Pieces, and two large sodas. I pay and walk toward the group, balancing the tray of food as I pull sips from her soda. She turns, sees the food, and her eyes grow wide.

"You're a genius," she says.

Gorging ourselves at the base of the bleachers, we halfheartedly watch the football game. The crowd squeals and boos as the ball satisfies and disappoints. A chill whispers through the air with the wind.

Halfway through her container of nachos Tiffany turns to me and says, "You're my best friend."

"Ditto," I say.

Our team loses in the final play. A lot of people boo, but I have a handful of Reese's Pieces left, so I focus on that.

"I wish you'd come to the dance," Tiffany says, walking me back to my car.

"Aren't you going with Mark?"

She frowns. I know if I just went she would dance with me – maybe we'd even make out – so I get in my car and say from the window, "Call me tonight if you want."

I leave the window down on the drive home, letting the night freeze the air in my car, my fingers burning against the wheel.

When I get home I pull a handle of bourbon from my father's liquor cabinet and pour twenty ounces of it into a Mountain Dew bottle. James once told me I could water down the remaining alcohol to make the bottle look full, but my father would be angrier if I ruined his whisky than he would be if I just took it. Plus, I'd have to find a funnel and the whole process seems exhausting, so I just put the jug back half empty.

On my back porch, I throw the soda bottle onto the roof. It rolls off and lands at my feet. Holding the bottle between my teeth, I stack a pile of logs from my father's woodpile up against the house, then climb onto the roof, lie back against it, and light a cigarette. I spend the next few hours drinking and staring at the stars, wishing I could recognize any of the constellations.

FIFTEEN

"Are you sure you want to go out in this?" Mom asks from the doorway, holding her palm skyward to collect falling snowflakes.

"The roads are only going to be bad in our neighborhood," I say as I maneuver down the porch steps.

"Watch out for patches of ice, please," she says and retreats into the house.

I start my car and let it warm up as I scrape the snow from my windows. "White Christmas" plays on the radio; since the day after Thanksgiving, Christmas songs have played on repeat everywhere I've gone. After the engine warms up, I back over a heap of snow and start slowly out of my neighborhood.

"White Christmas" gives way to "Last Christmas." I change the station and a DJ promises a solid hour of Christmas songs. I turn the radio off. Every Christmas song just reminds me that I'm going to spend this one without Valerie.

Tiffany made plans for us to meet her friends and I'm already late, so I speed past the cars inching along the highway. A thin layer of snow, blowing back and forth in the wind, wisps along the asphalt like a hundred snakes in tandem. A slow-moving car pulls into my lane, cutting me off, its hazard lights blinking their 'fuck off,' so I yank my car into the other lane to avoid a collision and my tires catch in the snow, dragging me onto the shoulder.

I push the accelerator and my tires spin out. Beside me, nearly obscured by the snow, a semi-truck sits on its side. Wrapped in destroyed evergreens with its lights flashing red and white, the truck looks like an apocalyptic Christmas tree.

I take a deep breath, turn my hazard lights on, and idle out of the snow.

I inch down Tiffany's iced-over road and park on what I think is her curb. Her mom welcomes me into their house, through the foyer, and into the living room.

"Do you want anything to drink?"

"Water, please."

"Sure you don't want something stronger?" I shake my head and she adds, "Let me know if you change your mind."

I sit still and awkward on the couch. I want to tell Tiffany I can't stay, but every minute I wait for her the roads get worse.

A wide-eyed boy, six or seven years old, peeks his head out from the hallway. He charges at me, head down like a rhino, when I look over, slamming his head into my stomach. I put my hand on his shoulder and hold him at arm's length.

"I know your dead girlfriend's name!" he shouts.

"Flynn!" his mom yells from the kitchen door as she emerges with a glass of water.

"What is it?" I play along.

"Valerie!" He cheers like a battle cry then barrel rolls around the room.

Tiffany parades up the stairs wearing jeans and a tight pink shirt. She sidesteps Flynn as he rolls toward her. He splays out on the floor, dragging his arms and legs on the carpet to make imaginary snow angels.

Seeing Tiffany catches me off guard and I feel myself smile.

"I haven't seen that in a while," she says.

"Have you looked outside?" I ask her, catching myself.

She opens the front door. "I knew it would snow."

"Why did you have me drive over then?"

"I wanted you to come." She answers like the question was idiotic.

"I need to leave before I'm stuck here."

"You can't drive in this," Tiffany's mom chirps from the kitchen. "Call your parents and tell them I want you to stay here tonight."

I look back at the road before I concede and, after calling Mom, follow Tiffany downstairs into her room where I crash on her bed, crushed under a strange sense of defeat. She turns on her TV and lies down next to me.

"It's nice to know I'm not going to have to wash my sheets when you leave."

"I'm sorry about that," I say, sitting up.

"I'm kidding. I'll probably still wash the sheets."

She laughs, so I do too.

"I'm glad you're stuck here," she says, reaching to run her fingers through my hair. I take her hand and gently set it on her lap before I slide off the edge of her bed to sit on the floor.

She lies out on the bed, props her head in her hands, and we watch a shitty romantic movie until her mother calls us to dinner.

Flynn fills his mouth with sauce and spits it on his plate, then he looks at me with a tomato-sauce smile. When I don't smile back at him, he climbs under the table and tries to pull my socks off.

After dinner Tiffany and her mom clear the table while I sit with Flynn.

"Do you want a beer?" Tiff's mom asks.

I look to Tiffany, who shrugs, and then I accept. Flynn darts out of the room when his mom hands me the drink, then returns with Candy Land.

"Tiffany and Brody don't want to play that right now, Flynn," Tiffany's mom says. Flynn pouts.

"I'll play," I say.

I don't know if he doesn't know the rules, doesn't understand them, or just likes to cheat, but sometimes he moves my pieces on his turn and just does whatever he wants. I let him.

"I'm ready for bed," Tiffany says mid-game, excusing herself from the table.

"Goodnight," I say, thinking I'll sleep on the couch.

She leans against the doorframe. "Coming?" I look awkwardly at her mom, who shoos me downstairs.

"You don't have to get beat up to spend the night with me," Tiffany says.

"I didn't know it was okay to stay in your room. I'll sleep on the floor."

"Why are you being so weird?" We walk into her bedroom. She puts her hands around my neck, her lips a breath away from being on mine, and says, "You've already slept in my bed, you know."

"Tiffany..."

She raises her eyebrows impatiently.

"I'm not-" I choke the words out, stumbling through them. "I'm going to make your life worse. I'm just... God dammit, I don't even know what I'm saying."

She leans in with her whole body to kiss me.

I can't help myself from thinking about Valerie. Our last kiss, the day she died. Cold and perfunctory.

Tiffany kisses me again so I kiss her back. I pour myself into her like I can't help it.

She moves her hands over my body as we make out, rubbing my neck and back. Then she takes my hands and places them on her breasts.

She kneels down and unbuttons my pants.

"Stop that," I say, pulling away from her. In an instant, all of the sexual tension is drained from me and replaced with anxiety. She must interpret my withdrawal as some kind of coy flirting because she grabs my pants and yanks them to the floor.

"What are these?" she gasps, looking up at me. She hesitantly rubs her finger over a long gash across my thigh.

"I don't want to have this conversation," I say as I pull my pants up to cover myself.

"God," she says with a whimper in her voice. "Did you do these to yourself?"

"Get off me." I turn to leave, but she grabs my wrist. I stare at her for a long time, hoping she'll just shut up and let it go. Outside, the snow is built up to her window. I'm not going anywhere.

"Yes." My voice is cold, almost hateful. There's a word for what I am, hurting myself: masochist. But more often people just replace it with "psycho." When people learn about my cutting, they change. Some freak out. Some stop talking to me all together. Some just care a little less.

Tiffany is the only person who I can talk to at all now, and my fear over being revealed a psycho is crippling because, whatever happens next, she and I won't be the same again.

She starts to cry, but unbuttons my pants again. I let her pull them off. Delicately, she rubs her fingers over the purple leather of my raised scars. "I've never seen scars this bad before."

Hypertrophic scars, they're called. Thick bands of red and purple scarring that spread down my thigh from so many nights of being a freak, not being able to keep it in. Each cut further separating me from anyone who could understand what it's like.

"They probably needed stitches."

I wait for her reaction, knowing the dreaded word is on her tongue – *psycho*: the word that will shatter our friendship. But it doesn't come – only tears. I don't know what to do, so I just stand against the window and watch her cry.

She turns off the light and takes my hand. We fall into her bed, and I lie next to her, stiff, waiting her out. She holds me close to her and whispers through her tears, "I'm so sorry."

"For what?"

"That you ever felt like you had to do that to yourself." She rubs her palm over my thigh. "I know some of these are fresh."

"Yeah."

"When did you start?"

"I don't want to talk about it."

"Please," she says. "You can trust me."

I hesitate before answering. "I was thirteen. My father used to kick the shit out of me." I regret the words as I say them, but I'm grateful just to have someone finally ask. "I mean, it wasn't any of the times he hurt me, it was the buildup. It was like every time he was mad at anything, especially my mom, he'd point it at me. But, this time, he didn't. He yelled at me, and I was ready for it. But he didn't hit me. He just left."

I take a deep breath, reliving that moment in my head. I was so tense. Frustration built inside me but there was no release.

"I hid in my room and just sat there seething, as hateful as I'd ever been." I was ready to hurt, and completely powerless. "The first time, I didn't even think about doing it. It was just an impulse. I had this little screwdriver and I just wanted to hurt so I stabbed it into my abdomen as hard as I could."

I take her fingers in my hand and run them along the scar on my side. "I was thirteen when I realized that I needed to hurt. Years of progression and you get these," I say as I run her fingers over the raised scars on my thigh, created in bursts of passion and hatred, with everything from my knives to shards of glass. "Truth is, without some kind of pain, things build up in me until I snap."

I don't mention that somewhere along the line I learned to love it.

"So you do it to be in control?"

"Sometimes. Sometimes I can't help it."

"Did Valerie know about it?"

I nod. "Oh yeah." She thought it was disgusting.

"Brody," she whispers.

"Yeah."

"I'm so sorry." She kisses my neck, her face still wet from her tears. I wrap my arms around her and kiss her forehead. We lie together for a long time, then I roll over and go to sleep.

In the morning I venture outside to dig my car out of the snow. Tiffany stands beside me, bundled up in thick winter clothes, drinking hot chocolate as I shovel.

"It's like we live in the fucking Yukon," I say as I hammer my fist into my driver-side window, shattering a thin layer of ice.

"Do you think you're going to the Winter Ball?" Tiffany asks, her words forming small wisps as they leave her mouth.

"I hadn't thought about it," I say, scraping the snow from my windshield. "Probably not."

"You should."

"With you?" I ask. I stop shoveling to watch for her answer.

"Well, I just thought we'd meet there."

I nod. "Yeah, okay." She kisses my cheek and walks inside.

I get in my car and start the engine. "Santa Baby" plays on the radio.

SIXTEEN

I dress in a gray suit, pink shirt, and striped, silk tie. I've been taking the Stackers that James gave me for a few weeks, usually before school, so I'm not surprised to see that I only have a third of the bottle left. I pop a few into my mouth, tongue the slick capsules, and swallow them dry. I dig a water bottle full of vodka out of my closet and use it to wash down another handful. Then, seeing that there are only a few left, I finish them off.

I catch myself smiling as I surrender my ticket and walk into the gym. It's done up with lights and glitter, but it's still a gym.

Tiffany, dressed in a gown cut from Cinderella's, stands at the other end of the room, laughing in the middle of a group of guys I don't know. I weave through the crowd, holding the corsage my mother bought.

She sees me walking toward her and excuses herself. I have to stop and take a breath before I say, "You look really pretty tonight."

She does. She is beautiful.

"What are you high on?" she says coldly.

"What?" I say as I slide the corsage over her gloved hand.

We dance to a slow song, her hands wrapped behind my neck, mine resting awkwardly above her ass. In a crowd of bodies, we are the only people who exist. She shuffles along with my feet, an exaggerated swaying.

My heart beats so fast that I can feel my pulse in my fingertips.

She looks up at me. I move in to kiss her and she tucks away. My lips feel tight and dry. Her eyes dart from side to side, then she gives me a look that says *Not here*. I look directly at her and rub my sandpaper tongue over the sticks of chalk protruding from my gums.

"You're freaking me out, Brody," she says. "What are you on?"

"Sorry," I say.

"Is it the same shit from Halloween?" she asks, her hands still around my neck.

"No." I stop swaying and suddenly the room feels full of strangers. "It's different shit."

"I can't deal with you like this."

"Sorry," I say. I step backward, away from the dance floor.

"Where are you going?" she asks.

"Excuse me," I mumble before I retreat to the bathroom. I check my face in the mirror, remembering what James told me about pulmonary edema. I can see my heartbeat in my neck. I should have read the recommended limit on the pill bottle; I should have at least counted the number of pills that I took.

I pee in short, second-long bursts and then throw up a blast of black slime. I prop myself against the toilet seat as I wretch. When I'm out of sludge to vomit I start dry heaving. My heart hurts like it's being crushed so I try to stand up but feel so dizzy that I sit on the closed toilet to avoid collapsing. I take deep breaths, kneeling in the stall on the bathroom floor, trying to slow my heart rate.

I wash my face and rinse my mouth out in the

sink. Then I walk back into the gym.

Nearly obscured by the crowd, Tiffany is dancing with Mark. The asshole runs his hands up her back and over her neck. Holds her too tightly. His hips press against hers. She smiles.

Chris spots me as I make my way to the door and he grabs my arm. "How have you been lately? Haven't seen you in a while."

"I'm fine," I say, shrugging my arm out of his grip.

His gaze shoots to Tiffany and then back to me. "You don't look fine."

I walk away from him without responding.

"Hey, man. New Year's Eve. Party at my house!" he yells as I walk out the door.

I let the cold run up my spine, all the windows down, as I speed home.

I'm never going to be good enough. Not for Valerie. Not for Tiffany. Not for anyone.

In my room, I pull the sacred pine box and what's left of a box of gauze out from under my bed, then I fold the ceremonial tools into a bath towel and take the processional walk to the bathroom.

I turn the shower on and strip. The bathroom fills with steam as I unclasp the box's metal latch, revealing the familiar handles housed in the bottom compartment and a magnetic strip glued to the top. Along the magnetic strip, fourteen blood- and rust-stained X-Acto knife tips are neatly aligned. I run my fingers over the blades, hesitating on the rusted utility blade, then a blood-caked keyhole saw blade. After some deliberation, I insert the concave carving blade into the thinnest chrome handle, screwing the fastener tightly so the blade won't catch in my skin.

I take a deep breath. Glide my fingers over the scars on my right thigh.

Self-injury requires a delicate mindset, a balancing act between self-loathing and unquenchable frustration. I need to hurt. I need to bleed. I need to open myself up before the pressure kills me.

I step into the shower.

My skin splits as the knife tears through it, unveiling fibers of muscle that quickly become obscured by a well of blood. Lightning strikes of pain bolt through my nerves. I raise the knife again and just as quickly lower it. And then again. And again. And again. Waves of searing pain spread through my body. I set the knife on the ledge of the tub and turn the hot water knob up as far as it will go.

SEVENTEEN

"Five!"

The countdown starts and everyone goes crazy.

"Four!"

I haven't talked to Tiffany in two weeks. I've called, but she's been out or busy.

"Three!"

Chris's basement is packed. The soccer team is here. So are some girls I know from school. Chris's fifteen-year-old sister Amy is here with a little group of drunk, giggling girls. Everyone yells at the TV as the numbers count down. Half the people in the room have dates. The other half have paired up. They're hugging and laughing and drinking.

"Two!"

It's so easy for them. They're quick to smile, easy to laugh. It's almost like no one told them how hard it is to care. They missed the lesson on how miserable life is.

"One!"

The ball drops. The crowd erupts, "Happy New Year!"

I watch Chris kiss his girlfriend. Everyone in the room is kissing. Amy pops out of nowhere and kisses me. Her little tongue finds its way into my mouth, and then she is back and giggling with her friends.

I call Tiffany again. She doesn't answer.

When Chris takes his girlfriend upstairs, I make out with his little sister.

EIGHTEEN

Mrs. Blanch hands me my English term paper from last semester, now marred with a blanket of red ink, before going over the syllabus with the new students. There's a uniform of disinterest in the room, which is common enough in school, but almost unavoidable in the last period of the day.

I flip through the paper, reading her sloppy, red script over typed text. *This is a rant*, one reads. *This doesn't have anything to do with the assignment.* On the last page I had drawn a man sawing off his own head with a hacksaw. Next to the drawing the red ink reads: *What happened to you?*

I drive home after school. Mom's asleep. My father's at work. I make a peanut butter and jelly sandwich and sit down to check my email. One message, from Tiffany: `How are you? Why haven't you been answering your phone? Call me.` I delete it like every other email she's sent since the New Year. Then I set my alarm clock for six p.m. and take a nap.

I roll out of bed to the sound of the alarm, then trudge to the bathroom where I shave and take a shower. After I dress, I drive downtown to meet Cheryl, who I haven't seen since art ended last semester.

I'm late by almost half an hour when I pull into a

kitschy theme park of a restaurant done up like a permanent garage sale. A hostess leads me to Cheryl.

"Sorry I'm late," I say and sit down.

"I'm glad." She smiles at me and brushes a lock of hair off her face. "I was a little late coming from work. I even changed clothes while I was driving over."

I take note of her t-shirt. "You work at a bank, right?"

"Yeah."

I pick up the menu and look it over as I say, "Why didn't you just wear the same clothes?"

"I wanted to relax." Her smile catches me off guard.

"So bad that you changed your clothes while you were driving? That sounds totally safe."

"Are you mad you weren't there?"

Knowing I can't say anything right to that, I grab the waitress and order water and a bacon cheeseburger. Cheryl orders a portobello wrap and diet soda.

"So, you just ordered a giant mushroom?"

She giggles. "What of it?"

"I'm curious and disgusted."

"You can try it if you're feeling brave."

Normally I'm happy to be around Cheryl. She's cute and funny and nice, but being *out* makes the air in the restaurant cling to my skin like cellophane. Every noise – every fork clinking against a plate, every too-loud conversation – is driving me crazy and suddenly I feel like my father on any given night he complains about how my mom's voice sounds like a power drill.

Cheryl smiles at me over her soda.

All my gears work overtime to smile back.

After dinner we go to the park and make out in her car.

In my room at home I take my shirt off and lie down to sleep. I toss against my sheets, feeling restless and manic. Valerie's picture frame, glass broken from where I cracked it to remove her photo, sits on my dresser facing me. I repeat the last conversation I had with Valerie in my head.

"Just promise me you'll drive safe," I demanded, knowing she was upset.

"Brody," she said, her voice cold, "anything that happens now is your fault."

I sat on my bed and waited for Valerie to call like she always did when she got home. After an hour I turned my light off and went to sleep.

My parents woke me knocking at the door. Mom eased it open. She and my father stood in my doorframe like *American Gothic*.

"What?" I hissed.

"Honey," my mother whispered. Maybe she didn't want to hear herself say it. "Honey, Valerie's been in an accident."

I leapt out of bed, instantly awake. "Take me to her," I snapped as I pulled a shirt over my head. Both of them stood in place with no sense of urgency, their eyes red and swollen, my father choking back tears.

"We can't," Mom said.

I felt hollow all at once, drained. I knew before she said it.

"Honey, she's dead."

I stand up from my bed and walk to the bathroom where I immediately kneel and throw up. I have to puke, to purge the meal completely. I strip and turn the shower on to drown out the sound, then I kneel again and shove my fingers into my uvula.

I throw up in bursts; first in watery blasts of

colorful liquids and chunks of French fries, then in solid, slimy chunks of hamburger meat and Cheryl's fried green tomato appetizer.

I'm still fingering my uvula when the door opens, startling me, so I jerk to the side just as a blast of vomit erupts from my mouth. Mom stands in the doorway, seeing me naked, crying, and covered in vomit.

I compose myself, look back at her, wide-eyed and smiling, and say, "Is there something I can help you with?"

NINETEEN

"Your mom tells me she's very worried about you," my psychiatrist says through his Brillo Pad beard. I fidget. He crosses then uncrosses his legs. "She says you've been making yourself throw up."

I look at him blankly.

"How long has it been? That you've been bulimic?"

We stare at each other for half an hour, him asking me questions that I don't answer, me not answering questions that don't have anything to do with what's happening inside of me.

"Are you finding it difficult to concentrate at school?" he asks.

I don't mention that I'm a powder keg. That I feel closer to spontaneous combustion every day.

"Do you still think about hurting yourself?" he asks.

I don't tell him that I want to bleed to death. That I think about it all the time and just can't bring myself to do it yet.

"Well, that's all the time we have for today," he says, tapping his finger on his watch. When I leave his office his secretary asks me when I'm available for my next appointment.

"I'm cured," I say, my face drained.

"Won't be needing this then," she says as she sets

a date book back on her desk. She traps me in a terrifying staring contest, smiling at me in a sick, plastic way. I try to match her smile, hoping mine doesn't look as fake. Her smile becomes unbearable.

"Here's your receipt," she says, handing it to me. Next to "diagnostic impression," where it had always been blank, are the numbers 301.83. I crumple it and throw it in the trash on my way out the door.

I crash on my bed and stare at the conglomerate of dead bugs in my ceiling fan light fixture. The phone rings.

"Hello," I croak.

"Hi." It's Tiffany.

"I don't have anything to say to you."

"I guessed that by the way you're ignoring me. I just want to know you're okay."

A bug flies into the light fixture. Its skin crackles when it touches the bulb.

"I'm not."

Silence. The bug circles the light.

"It's been like six months and everyone pretends I'm supposed to be fine," I say. "I feel like I'm about to explode any second. But I don't want to talk about it. And I don't want to talk to you."

"You can call me or come over if you change your mind. I'll always be here for you."

The bug lands in the mass grave with the other bugs, and I don't see it move again.

TWENTY

Chicago plays on Cheryl's face as she leans over to kiss me. I kiss her back and don my costumed smile and try to watch the rest of the movie, checking my watch constantly. The movie drags. I sigh with relief when its credits roll.

"What a good movie," Cheryl says as we leave the theater. It's snowing. A thin white layer of frost clings to everything.

"Are you kidding? That sucked." I open her door for her. "Literally the worst movie I've ever seen."

"Well, it had some really good parts."

Before I can start the car, she hugs me and showers me with long, open-mouthed kisses. She sucks my breath for air. Her hands push into my chest. She keeps kissing me even though I stop kissing her.

I pull away to ask, "Do you want to get some coffee?"

Her smile spreads so sincerely. In the soft overhead light of my car I look at her and realize she's really pretty. On the drive to Starbucks I consider why I can't bring myself to care about her.

We walk in and I order black coffee and she orders some crushed ice mess. I get my coffee first and, when I know she can't see, I swish it in my mouth and almost gargle.

She smiles from the counter.

"I just love coffee," she says after she sits down. "This was a good idea." She leans forward and cups her chin in her hands as we talk. She's so sweet, listening to every word I say. I take a deep breath, fearing that after a few dates she'll say something devastating: that she loves me.

I excuse myself to the bathroom and I sit in the stall, counting off the seconds on my watch for two full minutes before I take a long, deep breath of freedom and trudge back to the table.

She keeps talking about cavemen or cave drawings or something and I can't fucking stand it, so I drag her back to my car and we make out until I take her home.

When I get home, I throw my coat on the floor and go downstairs to the bathroom. I splash hot water on my face and then brush my teeth viciously. When I spit, a bright string of blood circles the drain.

My father walks down the stairs; just hearing his footsteps is enough to set me on edge. I wash the brush out, reapply the toothpaste, and scrub even harder.

"I got a call about your grades today," he says in a low, demanding tone. "We had this conversation."

"I don't care," I scoff.

"I'm not going to baby you the way your mother does. You're going to be out of this house the day you graduate. I'm not going to put up with your attitude. "

"If you want me out so fucking bad then I'll leave right now."

"Don't you dare use that language with me," he says, his voice raising. Pressure builds in my brain, a vice grip tightening. I know where this is going: where it always goes.

"Or what?" I know 'or what.' I've had seventeen

years to learn.

"If you think you can talk to me like that in my own house..." His face tightens and he clenches his fists. His voice is incendiary, pushing me closer to explosion with every word. I push past him toward the front door, but he grabs my shoulder and pulls me back so we're face to face. "Where do you think you're going?"

"Fuck you!" I snarl through clenched teeth.

He grabs my wrist and backhands me across the face. My brain goes white hot. I feel myself screaming at the top of my lungs. I punch a hole through the drywall. Seeing the fist-sized hole in the wall, I'm washed with embarrassment and then rage. My father's voice drowns out against my own screaming. I hammer my fist down, shredding the drywall.

I bound up the stairs and snatch my jacket off the floor, slamming the front door behind me as I run out into the snow. My mother appears in the doorway as I rev my engine and pull out into the yard, not bothering to back up. The tires catch the snow and lose traction. I mount a curb as I tear through my neighbors' yards. I slam into a trash can, garbage and snowflakes falling behind me as I race out of the neighborhood.

TWENTY-ONE

It's past midnight when I get to the cemetery. I stand on the hood of my car and climb over the spikes of the cast iron railing, falling hard on the other side. I trudge through the graveyard. My steps are the only ones staining the perfect blanket of snow. I walk through rows of headstones, brushing off the shell of white frost that obscures each name. I grow more frustrated with each stone, and I'm fighting tears by the time I brush the snow off and find hers.

This is the first time I've visited her since the funeral.

It was a Catholic funeral. I sat next to her cold, unflinching mother whose mouth tensed into a constant pucker. The face of a woman who had more fear of judgment than she had grief. She looked at me with a kind of emptiness that I'd rarely seen. I knew she blamed me, and I couldn't blame her.

Her face didn't move during the sermon. A perfect counterpoint to Valerie's father, a wet, sloppy ball of tears, overwhelmed by his loss.

The priest talked about her in the past tense. I had to excuse myself to throw up.

At the grave site after the service, the priest blessed her and repeated a prayer. The other Catholics mouthed the words. "... and it is in dying that we are born to eternal life." They lowered her casket, and she was gone.

Eternal life.

Your loved ones will live on forever. As bones.

In heavy gasps I fill my lungs with ice. I rub my hand over the stone. On the back I find grooves, more lettering: her initials engraved in a heart with my own. My gasps increase, my sobbing powerful, a force of nature.

Snow melts against my body heat and soaks into my clothes. I stay until the snow blankets the grave again, and it sits anonymous against the winterscape of the graveyard.

TWENTY-TWO

"What are you doing out here in the cold, boss?" Puck asks as he opens his front door. He looks from side to side. "Get on in here."

He pulls me into the house and I see that he has set up some furniture – cheap cardboard cutouts of bookshelves and an entertainment center. "How may I be of assistance in the middle of this cold-ass night?"

"I can't go home," I say, "and I need something to hold me over until I can."

He nods his head as I talk, and for some reason I know he gets it. I can tell he's had his share of nights where he couldn't go home.

"Can I score some painkillers?" I ask. "And maybe some weed?"

"Of course, dude. Take a seat." I sit on his plush, leather couch as Puck disappears into the hallway. I've been nervous about meeting with him, not knowing if my falling out with James had carried over to him, too. But he reappears with two baggies and drags a small coffee table against the couch where he sits with me and starts rolling a joint, so I figure he and I are good.

"Could you show me how to do that?" I ask. "I'm not very good at it."

"Sure, buddy." He repeats his steps on a second

joint, then lights it and says, "You try." I emulate his form. When I light it, before I can inhale, the bottom falls out of the cigarette, carpeting my lap with weed. Puck laughs like a horse. I sigh, defeated, and give up.

"I'll roll them for you this time," he says, passing his lit joint to me while he rolls. "Hey," he says after finishing one, "you heard outta James lately?"

I shake my head.

"You see him, you tell him he better get his ass over here. He'll know what I'm talking about."

I say that I will, knowing that I won't.

TWENTY-THREE

"Skip school with me today?" I ask Chris over the phone.

Normally I'm not up this early, but my father woke me up before he went to work to wish me happy birthday. Like every fight before, we just pretend it didn't happen. The hole in the wall was fixed before I ever came home. Neither of us said a word about it.

"Why would you even ask me to do that?" Chris says. "I'm on my way out the door anyway." He hangs up. I open my blinds and look through the dew-covered window.

Everything looks wet in the morning whether it rains or not.

I call Nolan. "Skip school with me today," I say.

"Sure, man." he says. "Happy birthday."

Nolan and I meet at a café for pancakes. He turned eighteen two months ago, so I look to him for advice on how to enjoy my newfound adulthood.

"Porn. Tattoos. Cigarettes," he says, raising his fingers like bullet points while he talks. He shovels in a bite of pancake. "Oh, yeah. And you've gotta sign up for the draft."

"Is that what you did?" I roll a pancake into a tube and dip it in butter. "You spent your eighteenth birthday signing up for the draft?"

"It's your civic duty," he says with a smile.

"I can't tell if you're joking," I say as I wave the waitress over for the check. "Oh, I can drop out of school as of today, too."

"I don't need to tell you how fucking dumb that would be."

"What's the point?" I ask, covering another rolled pancake in butter.

"Just try to enjoy your birthday, man. One day without pondering the meaning of existence, okay?" He reaches for the check. "This is on me. Happy birthday. Anyway, porn, tattoos, or cigarettes first?"

We each buy a pack of cigarettes at the gas station by the café, sit outside and smoke them. I light two and smoke them at the same time, hot-boxing them. Nolan takes this as a challenge, lights three. I stuff the rest of the pack in my mouth and light them, letting them burn down to their filters while I stare at people entering the gas station. I try not to laugh, but I can't help it and I choke a little when I do.

Next stop: porn. The attendant doesn't even look at me as I walk through the door. I stand at the counter, waiting for him to ID me. Nolan walks by to peruse the videos. I give up on the attendant and meet Nolan in the 99-cent section.

"You're even cheap when it comes to porn?"

"I'm a value shopper," he says, prideful. "Check this one out." He hands me a video called *Trailer Trash Dungeon Porn*.

"That cuts to the point, doesn't it?" I look through the other titles. One catches me off guard: *Feet and Meat*. On its cover, fully-clothed girls step in raw hamburger meat. I hand it to Nolan. "Look at this shit."

He stares at it for a long time, flipping it over to read the back, then says "Gross" and buys it.

Next: tattoos.

"What can I do you for?" an artist asks when we

walk in. He is lost in long waves of matted hair that obscure his stringy body and faded tattoos.

"I don't know," I say. "I want a tattoo." His arm is a billboard, an amalgamation of pop stars and product logos. Each of his tattoos is worse than the last.

"You should probably think about it first," Nolan says, "but I know what I want."

"There's a forty-dollar set-up fee," the artist says to Nolan as he hands me a portfolio. "Let me know when you pick one out."

He waves Nolan back to what feels like a barber's booth and I flip through page after page of bad tattoos: '70s cartoons, zodiac signs, a tractor mowing over a sports team mascot. The buzz of the tattoo gun hums like soothing white noise as Nolan gets two black crosses inked above his elbows.

"What about you, birthday boy? Do you want to permanently mar your body on a whim?" Nolan asks as he sits up and inspects his tattoos.

"I'm going to hold off," I say. "Maybe next time."

Mom is waiting for me at the door when Nolan drops me off. I smile at her, but her face is locked in a scowl and I realize it was a mistake to come home at all.

"Where have you been?" she asks as I walk into the house.

"Out, clearly," I say, taking my jacket off.

"You didn't think you should tell me you weren't going to be home for dinner?"

"Leave me alone. I don't need this."

"You don't need to spend your birthday with your family?"

"I don't need to feel guilty about every fucking thing I do."

"Get upstairs. We ate already. Your father's been waiting for you to cut the cake."

"I don't want cake," I say. My stomach is already

getting hot, my brain already tightening.

"I don't care if you want cake or not. Get upstairs."

"No." I walk toward my room.

"Your birthday's not just for you. It's for your family," Mom says, her voice heavy and disappointed. "Get upstairs and eat a piece of cake. I don't care if you like it or not." I turn around and stomp upstairs to sit at the table, silently stewing. Mom sits down and lights the candles.

"Did you have a good day?" my father asks. If I weren't already on edge, his voice would be enough to put me there.

"Until I got home," I say.

Mom starts singing to cut me off. "Happy birthday to you..."

My frustration rises with every word of the song. If they gave a shit about how I feel this obligatory bullshit wouldn't be happening. I don't even like cake.

"Fuck you!" I shout over her.

"Happy birthday to you!" she continues.

"Fuck this." I knock the chair backwards as I stand up. She's still singing as I walk out of the dining room.

"Get back here, you ingrate!" Mom yells, cutting her song short.

I stomp down the stairs and grab my jacket.

"If you leave this house then you better just not come back!" she screams, half crying, as I slam the door behind me.

TWENTY-FOUR

I stop at a green light on a one-lane street, letting cars build up behind me. When the light turns red, I slam the gas pedal to the floor. My car yanks away from me. I steady it and disappear down a parallel street where I get caught behind a van at another stop light so I punch my dashboard, smashing my fist into the air conditioner vents until they shatter, leaving flaps of skin hanging from the cuts on my knuckles. I punch my steering wheel repeatedly until the van lurches forward and I rip the vent covers out of the dashboard and throw them out the window.

My eyes well over and tears stream down my face. I sob so hard I can't breathe, so I pull into an abandoned parking lot and lay my head on the steering wheel.

I used to tell Valerie about shit like this. She used to help me keep it in.

If anyone but Valerie had died she'd have been there to pick up the pieces. Nolan or Chris or my parents or fucking anyone else could have died. But it was Valerie.

I pull off my jacket and drop it on the floorboard. Then I take my pocket knife, flick the blade up with my thumb, and dig it into my left forearm. I growl as it rips into my skin. Blood oozes down my arm into the bend of my elbow and drips onto my pants.

I dig in again, cutting deep and slow.

I carve to the muscle, through a layer of tiny, white, fatty globs. When the skin gives, the cut doesn't bleed right away; it's a delayed reaction until all at once the wound fills with blood and drools down my arm. I breathe deep, exhale, let the pain transform me.

I look out into the parking lot as I reach down for my jacket. Then I catch my ragged, watery face in the rearview mirror and realize that I'm actually insane; I'm sitting in an abandoned parking lot in the middle of the night on my birthday tearing my skin apart and bleeding all over myself because I couldn't handle eating cake with my parents.

These new cuts, deep and flush with blood, I will never be able to hide. I'll wear these scars like a badge, a constant reminder to myself and to anyone who sees them that I can't control myself. These scars will yell proudly to strangers, *Yes, I am insane. I am not like you. Do not trust me.*

I put the jacket back on. Blood saturates it immediately and the crook of my elbow feels coated in slime. I look at myself again in the mirror, wondering why I can't just function like everyone else.

I drive to Tiffany's neighborhood and park a few houses up. I tremble as I walk through her neighbor's yard, my teeth chattering in the warm spring night. Her house feels a thousand miles away, but I don't really have anywhere else to go like this. I couldn't just show up at Nolan's covered in blood. Any hospital would take one look and have me committed. And there's no way I can go home.

I stumble through the last few steps and fall down at her window. I prop myself up against it and start to cry again. She knows about my cutting, but it's one thing to know about it and another to see it. I knock hard on the glass, knowing that if she doesn't answer I'm fucked.

Then I realize she might not even be here. I haven't talked to her in weeks. She could be out. She could have a boyfriend.

She could have two or three.

I knock again on the window, but I don't feel quite as hopeful about it.

The room lights up. She draws back her curtains and I can see the gears moving in her head. Her expression twists from excited to terrified. She focuses on my arm and gasps, rushing to open the window.

I must look so fucked.

"Hurry," she says as she motions me inside.

She grabs my elbow to help steady me as I crawl through the window, but I fall anyway. I grab her leg and pull myself up slowly.

"Oh. My. God," she gasps and pulls her hand away, her palm greased with thick, congealing gore. "What happened? Who does this shit to you?"

My eyes well up.

"Let me get dressed and I'll take you to the hospital." She's wearing a long t-shirt and nothing else. As smooth as her legs are, I can't focus on anything but the urgency in her voice.

"I can't go to the hospital," I say, carefully pulling my arm out of the bloody sleeve. "They'll know I did this to myself."

Tears well up in her eyes as she starts to cry.

"I'm a piece of shit, okay?"

She grabs the back of my head and forces me to look at her. "Don't you say that and expect me to help you." She walks into the bathroom and washes her hands, then returns with a box of Band-Aids and a damp cloth. "Give me your arm."

She wipes some of the blood from my arm,

unveiling the wounds. "These aren't going to be worth shit," she says as she tosses the Band-Aids on the floor. "Wait right here and don't bleed on anything."

I nod.

She walks upstairs and I squeeze my bicep to try to minimize the blood flow. She doesn't deserve this shit. No one does.

She comes back with an armful of supplies. "Okay," she says, "put your arm under the sink." She runs water over it first, then rubs it down with alcohol before she covers the wounds with gauze and then wraps my arm tightly with an elastic bandage from a roll.

"How do you know how to do that?" I ask, relieved.

"I don't. I've never done it before." She stuffs the remnants in a plastic bag with my jacket. "That's garbage now." Then she grabs my mummified arm and pulls me onto her bed with her. "Why did you do that, Brody?"

"I told you. I'm a piece of shit." I turn away from her.

"If you want to stay here you need to stop saying that." She lies next to me, her hand on my chest. "Just tell me. Just get it out. You can talk to me."

"I'm," I breathe in deep, "I'm just. Anything sets me off. I just-" I start to cry as I'm talking, and I realize how fucking sick I am of crying. "I just can't deal with fucking anything. I'm not good enough for anyone. I wish I was dead."

"Don't say that. You're good enough." She nuzzles her head into the crook of my neck. "And I'm glad you're not dead."

"Why wasn't I good enough for you?"

"What are you talking about?"

"Like at the dance." I keep my head turned away

from her.

"You mean the dance where you showed up high and left me there without even saying you were going?"

"Never mind." I turn away from her.

"Brody, I love you. You're a dick, but I love you."

I let that sink in.

I know what I'm getting into. I know who she is, who she's been. I know I'm not safe with her. Even asking sets me up for destruction.

"Tiffany, do you want to be my girlfriend?"

She cups my face in her palms and kisses me.

"Yes. But you have to stop hurting yourself. I can't see you like this anymore. Can you do that for me?"

"I'll try," I say, and part of me really means it.

TWENTY-FIVE

Her parents don't even ask what happened, why I'm there.

I sneak back into my house through my window to get clothes and books and my drugs, careful not to take more than I could bring back in one trip.

I stay at Tiff's through the week, sleeping in her bed, eating dinner with her. It's awkward at first, but I can't bring myself to go home. Her parents are too nice to me, but I'm afraid one of them is going to bring up how long I've stayed and ask me to leave so I go out of my way to avoid them if I can. Sometimes I go out for a milkshake or to buy pot and when I come back I just sit in my car on the street and listen to the radio, waiting as long as I can before I go in.

Around the second week, I start driving Tiffany to school and I lie in bed with her at night while she does her homework. Her commitment to school makes it easy to study. Her schedule makes it easy to sleep.

When in Rome.

In May, two weeks from graduation, Tiffany's dad takes us to the Derby because he got box seats through his work. He buys me and Tiffany mint juleps and we sip them while he drinks scotch. Tiff and her mom critique hats they think are trashy, but none of them seem much different from the hats they're wearing: gigantic brims with lush, vibrant flowers. It's a blistering hot day, but Tiffany's dad leaves his blazer on, so I do, too.

"And whom do we have for the race?" Tiff's father asks. I've lived in Kentucky my whole life, but have never been to a horse race before.

"Who's racing?" I ask.

He hands me a betting form with the horses' ridiculous names and some triangles. After careful deliberation over which horse's name I like the most, I point and say, "This one."

"Which one?" He's drawn in, all business.

"It was a toss-up between Ten Most Wanted and Domestic Dispute, so I went with Funny Cide."

"Alright," he says, "Funny Cide it is." He scribbles frantically and hands the form to a waiter along with a large wad of cash. "I have a grand on your horse."

The day drags on, getting hotter and stickier with every syrupy julep. Several horse races flash by, only a few minutes each, but the most exciting spectacles are the people. From our box seat, elevated above the pit, we watch:

A man stumbles into another man, who is offended, so the offender punches him, and he punches back, and they push each other back and forth until huge men in black shirts carry them away;

A woman screams at her lover, calls him a liar, and stomps away;

This leads to the main event, which happens without warning when a little boy unscrews the cap from a bottle of Pepsi and pours it out on his sister's head.

The eponymous prize race passes with much fanfare: *go-boy-go*s and a lot of screaming. The crowd is alive. This race is much more important than the previous ones; for two minutes the fate of the world rests on these golden horses. I even catch myself getting excited when Funny Cide passes Empire Maker and wins.

Tiffany's dad grabs me tight around my shoulders as he collects his winnings – more than twenty grand – and gives me five hundred dollars with a "Thanks for the tip, son."

I graciously accept my earnings, a fair day's pay for the exhaustion and heat I've endured. There's talk of after-party celebration. Tiffany and I, being much too young to party, stumble drunk out of Churchill Downs and into the back of a taxi. The taxi drives us back to her parents' house where we have sex on her living room floor.

TWENTY-SIX

The last two weeks of school are a blur of "I'll miss you" and "Where are you going to college?" I apply to all the schools that Tiffany does. I want to be done with high school and move on, so I borrow notes and read the text books and study to ace my finals. It's enough – I checked – to pull me through with Cs and Ds.

Mrs. Blanch smiles when I hand her my term paper again. "Did you make it easier on me this time?" she jokes.

"I took out all the cuss words." I smile at her, caught up in the excitement of finishing school and starting something new.

Everything in the last week is preparation. We practice the graduation ceremony. We say our goodbyes and good riddance. People I don't know hand me their yearbooks and I write encouraging things and draw little pictures.

I keep an eye out for James. A wave of sentimentality gets the better of me; I want to wish him the best and get it off my conscience. I hang around his locker and ask around, but no one's seen him. I hear he's dropped out of school, but that doesn't make sense. Druggie or not, he's way smarter than anyone else I know.

On the last day of school Tiffany meets me at

lunch. We eat together and flip through her yearbook. A Sharpie heart borders my picture. I point to it with two fingers and ask, "You like me, huh?"

I start to flip the next page, but she closes the book and says "I love you, stupid" before she kisses me in the middle of the lunchroom.

There is a light that shines through the fog. And, in the same way an action becomes a memory, we graduate.

TWENTY-SEVEN

Someone is screaming. I can't make out the words. I can't hear anything over the screaming.

I wake violently, jarred to consciousness by a claw closing around my left calf. I howl. My body clenches, reeling from pain like I've never felt.
  Tiffany, crying, gasps in short exasperated breaths. "Everything is going to be okay."
  I want to look back to where I hear her voice, but I can't move my head or my arms or anything.

I stir, awakening to a faceless doctor rubbing a sonogram machine against my stomach. Tiffany, seeing I'm awake, grabs my wrist.
  "Am I pregnant?" I rasp.
  "I'm checking for internal bleeding," the doctor announces to no one.
  Tiffany's eyes are swollen. Makeup is stained across her face.
  "Is it a boy?"
  She giggles, maybe stops crying for a second. I can't tell.
  I close my eyes, focusing on her hand in mine, and say, "I've always wanted a boy."
  The doctor says something inaudible and Tiffany starts crying again.

TWENTY-EIGHT

I sit up slowly and notice the tubes in my nose. I pull them out. They're shallow, just long enough to plug into my nostrils. I take a deep breath. Exhale. Repeat.

A large, three-paned window bathes me in sunlight. The room is a sterile hospital room like a TV set with beeping props, and I can't focus past the buzz of electronics, the high-pitched drone.

Tubes slither from my wrists to a bag hung from a medical coat rack. I strain to focus long enough to see there are two bags, one marked MORPHINE.

My nose hurts to the touch. I rub my fingers into my face and watch dried, black blood flake off like dandruff. I shake the blood chips from my palm and search more intensely for damage.

I slide out from a paper hospital gown and survey my body. Aside from a large tube in my penis and some gauze wrapped around my left leg, I find nothing out of the ordinary. Convinced that my blood-covered face is the extent of the damage, I drop my legs over the edge of the bed and hop down, letting my full weight land all at once.

I immediately collapse into a pile on the floor and scream.

I've broken bones playing soccer. I've cut deep into my muscles. I've had the shit beaten out of me a handful of times.

I have never felt pain before this.

Something inside my body. Nerves melting. Shut down.

I clamor to pull myself back onto the bed, but my leg twists and contorts every time I move.

I scream again.

Two nurses rush into the room. With their help I pull myself back onto the bed. My left leg is covered in gauze, and black blood creeps through it like death. Groaning in agony, I shout at the nurses. "Where's Tiffany?"

The first nurse handles the bag of morphine while the other nurse unwraps the blood-soaked gauze. Just then, as if she senses my terror, Mom walks in.

"What happened?" I ask.

She holds my hand in hers. "You got hit by a drunk driver in an SUV, sweetie."

"How long have I been here?"

"Three days."

The nurses, both standing over my leg, peel back the last length of medical tape. Under the bandage my leg is sliced open on both sides. The wounds are maybe ten inches long and an inch deep. One side is stitched closed with rubber bands. The other is gaping, a snapped rubber band still threaded through my skin. It hangs open, blood drooling out.

Warmth washes over me and I start to breathe. The nurse pulls blood-soaked paper towels from the wound and packs it with saline-soaked replacements. This is fascinating at first, like watching a documentary about processing deer meat, but quickly becomes boring.

"Why does my leg look like hamburger meat?" I ask calmly, meditative.

"It shattered in the wreck," Mom tells me. I watch her mouth move, but she isn't in the same room.

Far away. Farther and farther.

"You have a titanium rod in your shin. You're lucky, really. You could have lost your..."

TWENTY-NINE

A nurse wakes me up when she comes into my room to place a tray of food on my bed.

Someone is always waking me up. Nurses come in and replace tubes and exchange empty bags for balloons filled with medicine or salt water or whatever. They never tell me what they're doing, and I can't pull myself together long enough to ask. I watch the nurses, but never quite focus. Sometimes I want to ask them questions, about anything or maybe just their names, but words float around my head like fireflies. Sometimes I grasp one and crush it. Other times I catch one gently and hold it tightly in my palm, but it escapes before I manage to catch another one.

Occasionally a nurse walks in and turns on the TV. Sometimes a different nurse comes in and watches it.

I wake to a completely dark room. I flip the TV on, find the weather station and see that it's one in the morning. I haven't talked to Tiffany since I've been in the hospital, so I call her, hoping that, if she's asleep, she'll understand me waking her up. I get a busy signal, so I hang up and call back. Busy.

A doctor walks in and turns the light on. He hovers at the edge of my bed, so I hang the phone up.

He writes something on his chart, then watches my face as he unwraps the bandage around my calf. He rubs his thumb down my shin. When I don't move he pushes harder, digs his fingernail in. I pull my lip back, snarling silently. He stops, looks at me for what feels like forever, and then halfheartedly wraps the bandage so it hangs loosely in its place around the black dust that has caked in thick chunks around my still-open wounds.

THIRTY

The sun sets heavy in my eyes as they adjust on Tiffany. For a moment I don't believe it's her, then she strokes my cheek with the back of her hand and says, "I've got you tonight."

I hold her hand against my heart and cry. I haven't been up for more than a few hours at a time in the week I've been in the hospital. Mom said that Tiff has visited, but I haven't seen or spoken to her since the wreck.

"How do you feel?" she asks.

I can't get a straight answer about my damage. I overheard a doctor saying things like spinal compression and compartment syndrome. Someone mentioned "shadows" on CAT scans of my brain, possible brain damage. But they keep telling me that I'll have to wait and see.

"I have a tube in my penis," I say.

She starts to cry in a silent, dramatic way like we're on a soap opera. This week is a special two-hour long episode of *Days of How Bad Your Life Sucks*, complete with medical drama, crying, amnesia. She lies down, careful to avoid putting any weight on me, and wraps her arms around my neck.

"I'm so sorry, baby," she says. "You remember anything?"

My memory is spotty. I don't remember going

shopping, which is apparently when a drunk driver hit Tiffany's car. I don't remember graduating the day before the wreck. I only remember blurs of motion, sometimes colors, and words out of context.

And being mad.

And screaming.

"No," I lie.

She cries harder. I kiss her nose and then her forehead, then pull her into me and say, "It's okay."

"This is my fault," she cries.

I hold her tighter.

"I was so scared. You were lying there, limp. I thought you were going to die."

"It's going to be okay. I'm okay."

"I don't know what I would do if you weren't." She looks at me with doe eyes, doesn't say anything, just holds my face with her palms and stares until she smiles through her tears and asks, "You have a tube in your penis?"

I laugh. "Yeah."

"Can I see it?"

THIRTY-ONE

They staple my leg closed. Pump staple after staple down the wounds like tiny metal ladders.

A few days later I sign some release forms and a nurse wheels me down to meet my parents. A titanium rod is stuffed in my shin bone. I talked to the surgeon for less than five minutes, but he explained that the rod would carry my weight and allow me to walk while the shards of my bone re-form around it.

Heat and exhaust form a thick, sticky layer of smog outside the hospital. My father pulls his car in front of the visitor's entrance. In two steps I could stand up from the wheelchair and crawl into the back seat of my father's sedan.

The last time I tried to walk I fainted in the recovery ward hallway. Three nurses struggled to pick my collapsed body up off the floor.

My discharge papers include six months of rehab.

The rod supports my weight. One of the nurses had initially said I wouldn't walk again for six months, but she was wrong. I stand up from the wheelchair and hold my crutches in one hand while I settle all of my weight on my feet.

Now or never – deal with the pain or be bedridden.

I step out with my left foot and crushing pain

shoots into my calf. I let the weight settle. The suffering stays sharp. A bead of sweat drips from my eyebrow, down my face, and into my mouth.

The only thing stopping me from walking now is my own pain tolerance. I step out with my right foot and an earthquake of agony convulses through my body. I quiver, bone shards vibrating around the rod.

Mom holds the back door open, watching to make sure I don't fall.

One more step.

Blood oozes down my leg, pumping through the wound's dressing. I grab the door and turn around, facing the nurse, and bend my knees to ease backwards into the seat.

My knees buckle.

Tendon damage: ACL, meniscus.

"Your tendons are basically destroyed," one of the doctors said during a hazy, late-night visit. "You're going to have two options: we can shave the tendons down or replace them with tendons donated from a cadaver."

Thanks to modern day necromancy I can walk with my knee full of zombie parts.

I catch myself on the door. Mom and the nurse both rush to my side. "I've got it," I say as I stand myself back up and ease in.

"How you doing, son?" my father asks from the driver's seat.

"Whatever doesn't kill you, right?" I answer. Or, whatever doesn't kill you cripples you for the rest of your life.

"That's the spirit," he says.

The pulsing in my knee wears down by the time we get to my parents' house, just in time for me to get out and do it again. It was just assumed that I'd come back here. No one mentioned the fight on my birthday, just like no one mentions any fight before it. As I slide out of his backseat, I secretly relish the long smear of blood I leave in my father's car.

I step up four concrete steps to the porch, then two steps to the front door. I wait while Mom finds her keys and opens the door, all the time balancing on my good leg. Then I take the two steps across the landing. She stands beside me as I take the five tiled steps down the stairs and fifteen steps along the hallway that leads to my bedroom. With every step I take, blood seeps from the wounds on either side of my leg.

The whole process, from car to bed, takes about half an hour.

Mom's hand rests on my shoulder as I settle onto my bed. When she notices that blood is soaking through my pants, she sighs, wearing an expression of defeat that I haven't seen since Valerie died.

"I'll get you a towel before I go get your prescriptions filled," she says as she palms my forehead. When she returns she brings me a glass of water and one of the opiates the doctor sent home. "Feel better, sweetie," she says before she kisses my check and leaves.

When she's gone I stash the pill in my desk drawer and pull my leg to my chest, breathing deeply as I learn to appreciate how much it hurts.

THIRTY-TWO

When I wake up my pajamas are stuck to my calf with my blood again. As I peel them off, thick globs of still-sticky blood stretch from my pants to my leg.

It's been four days. Four days of Mom bringing me every meal. Doling out my pain medicine one pill at a time.

Four days of staring at the stucco texture on my ceiling.

Four days of being bedridden.

I roll over and count the pain pills that I've stashed in my desk drawer. There are more than enough to dull the aching pain in my leg. There are enough to make me forget about pain, to make me feel like every cell in my body is floating.

I close the drawer and lie back, facing the ceiling.

Four days alone with nothing to do but think about why I lived and Valerie didn't.

I call Tiffany.

"Hi," she answers.

"Hey," I say.

"Oh, Brody. I'm kind of busy."

"With what?" I ask.

"My friend David is over."

I sit up and hang my legs off the edge of the bed. "Who?"

"You've never met him."

"So, your boyfriend is bedridden because of an accident you caused and you can't stop what you're doing long enough to see why I called?"

"Don't talk to me like that," she snaps.

"Don't call me again," I say.

"You don't call me again!" She slams the phone down.

"Fuck!" I yell, sitting up straighter. I call her back and the phone is busy so I wait ten seconds and call again. It's still busy so I slam my receiver down too and clench my fists. I sit, thinking about Tiffany in her room with some fuck I've never met.

Nothing is keeping me in bed but my own pain tolerance.

I naturally rest my weight on my good leg as I stand up, but shift so my left leg supports my frame. The pain is crushing, but I step out into the hall, leaving my crutches by the bed. I put my arm out, hand against the wall, and step forward on my metal bone. As the pain shudders through my body I steady myself and take another step.

At the end of the hall I turn around and start back to my room. Blood spits out with every step, and by the fourth lap my pants are soaked. I feel faint by the fifth lap, weak by the sixth. On the seventh, I pull my arms away from the wall and do my best to walk like a human, enduring every step.

THIRTY-THREE

A breeze leaks in through my open window as I flip through TV stations. I settle on a daytime talk show. The first story is about a school teacher and his adulterous wife. She fucks his students, apparently. The crowd boos.

"You don't know me!" she screams into the audience.

My phone rings.

"How'd your day go?" Tiffany asks.

This morning I woke up at six to spend three hours at triage before a doctor sucked two cups of blood and yellow fluid out of my swollen knee with a horse needle. Then he told me to stay off of it.

"Fine."

"Well," she segues, "we're going to eat, and my dad said you should get off your lazy ass and come with us."

On TV, Adulterous Wife is weeping. Saying she can't control herself.

"I'm sorry about the other day," I say. "I'll come if you pick me up."

"It's okay," she says. "We're leaving now."

I grunt in acknowledgment.

"I love you," she says.

I let that sink in before I hang up. The host offers to help Adulterous Wife get treatment. The show ends, and the station goes to a commercial break.

After hobbling to my closet to find a clean pair of pants, I sit down to change. I've been out of the hospital for three weeks, but this morning I dribbled blood out of my still-healing wound until a crimson racing stripe streaked down my khakis.

It's a relatively cool day for June, so we sit outside at this Cajun restaurant. I order a cheeseburger and Tiffany's dad holds his hand up like a traffic cop. "You can get a hamburger anywhere. Get the alligator." He orders the alligator. "And I'll have a beer," Tiff's dad says. "You want a beer, Broderick? Of course you do. Two beers."

The waiter gives him a vexed look, but smiles when Tiff's dad hands the menus back with a twenty-dollar bill on top.

"How's your leg?" Tiffany's mom asks. Flynn sits next to her playing a Game Boy. He stops playing when she asks this and looks at me, squinting against the sun.

"Good," I say. "I'm doing physical therapy. I'll be fine." Tiffany squeezes my thigh in support.

Three times a week I emasculate myself, balancing on rubber balls or ambling on a treadmill. The phrase 'learn to walk again' is bounced around sometimes, but I didn't forget how to walk. The only difference is that now I walk with a limp and take every step on shards of broken glass.

"That's really good," Tiff's mom says. Her dad nods in agreement.

"The worst part about the whole thing," I say, "is dealing with my lawyer."

They both laugh.

Nolan's dad recommended my lawyer. The first time I met with him I sat in his office – filled with stuffed birds – for half an hour while he rambled on about deep pockets and accountability like he was juggling chainsaws.

The waiter brings our food. "How hard would it be to bring us an extra chair?" I ask. He pulls one from an adjacent table and sets it next to me with a hand motion that says *voila*. I prop my leg up and eat.

THIRTY-FOUR

After a particularly boring physical therapy session, Tiffany comes over to watch a movie. Mom lets her in and I stand up when she walks through my door, holding myself up straight on both legs. She hugs me. Tanning lotion smells sweet against her skin.

"How's the leg?" she asks.

"Better all the time."

"I should sell you for glue." She drops her bags and holds my chest as I sit down. "'Cause you're a stallion. Get it?" She punches my shoulder. "Get it?"

I leaf through the DVDs she brought and pick *Jackass: The Movie* from her choices. She starts the movie and lies next to me over the blanket. We spoon during the first few gags; someone skateboards into a bush, someone chases a midget.

"I'm glad you're healing fast," Tiff says over her shoulder. She rubs her hand along my hip.

I breathe lightly into her hair. She rolls over and kisses me. We make out as I unbutton her pants and then she pulls the blanket over us and slides out of her jeans. She grips my back as we kiss, then rests her palm against my chest. "Baby, your heart is beating so fast."

I pull her in to me and kiss her as I struggle to take my pants off over my bandaged leg.

Someone knocks on my door.

"Fuck," Tiffany and I whisper in unison.

"Who is it?" I shout. Nolan walks in. "You know man, knocking doesn't count if you don't wait for me to let you in."

"What? It's not like you two were having sex." He sits down across from the bed on my desk chair. "I just dropped by to see how you were doing. Haven't seen you since you were in the hospital."

"I was doing pretty good," I say. Tiffany blushes at me and stifles a laugh.

"This *Jackass*? I haven't seen it yet." He turns to face the TV.

"Stay and watch it with us," she says. Her courtesy is mostly annoying. I should tell Nolan to fuck off so I can have sex, but I don't. We all watch the movie, Tiffany and I lying pantless under the blanket. Neither of us move during the entire movie. It's funny enough, crude in a way I can't help but laugh at, so it passes quickly.

When it's over, Nolan excuses himself. "Call me later, man," he says. "I'm not going to overstay my welcome." He winks at me on his way out the door.

THIRTY-FIVE

The lawyer calls with good news, so Mom drives me to his office where he's waiting with a check for $66,666.66. Apparently having one's bones ground into gelatin has a market value of $100,000.00, and when the lawyer called my father's insurance company they just sent a check. After taking his cut of $33,333.33 for making the phone call, the rest is mine.

Tiffany's parents are also insured in the same amount, and the lawyer assures me that a similar check will come at some future point. Then, he continues, I will sue the drunk driver and a third check will come in an as-of-yet-undetermined amount. This part, he tells me, will take years.

My health insurance covered my hospital stay, and I have no bills, so I take the sixty-six thousand dollars and deposit it into my checking account.

THIRTY-SIX

Tiff and I drive to an Indian restaurant where we meet Rachel and her new boyfriend, Rob. The weather is clear, so we let the hostess seat us on the patio. I prop my leg on Tiffany's knee as the waiter, a guy not much older than I am, asks for our drink orders. "I'll have a beer," I tell him. He cocks his head like I'm joking. I hand him a folded twenty-dollar bill, emulating Tiffany's dad.

"Me too," Rob says with a smug look, like he thought of it or paid for the waiter's dereliction. Rob is Samoan, I think, with a deep tan and an easy smile. I've never met a Samoan unless Rob is. Tiffany and Rachel order drinks and the four of us drink beer and eat samosas.

"So, what are you into?" Rob asks me, catching me off guard.

"Not much, I guess," I lie. Rob is nice enough, but I don't want to play the 'do you like what I like' game.

"Well, like, what kind of music do you like?" he asks again. It's the same question, but it isn't open-ended anymore.

"Oh, I like music," I say. "I mean, whatever's good." I take a long deliberate draw from the neck of my beer bottle.

"Man, music is my life!" He starts listing bands he likes – some I know and most I don't. His list drags on without any self-editing. I nod my head as he talks. Look him in the eye so he knows I'm listening. I start to dislike Rob.

Tiffany saves me and asks, "Do you guys want to go see a movie?"

Rob grabs my shoulder and bursts, "Let's go see a concert! There's a cool indie band playing at Headliners." He leaves his hand on my shoulder as he says this. Then he looks at me with a wide, amicable smile that says, *We are winning, buddy*.

"Standing room only," he adds.

I knew I should have told Rob that I hated music. I always pick the wrong answer.

Rachel agrees with Rob. She wants to go to the concert.

"What do you want to do, babe?" Tiff asks me. She knows I don't want to go, but she's polite. She can't say no, so I can't say no.

"It's cool," I lie. "Let's go." Tiffany smiles and squeezes my hand.

I regret leaving my crutches in my car.

THIRTY-SEVEN

"Are you sure about this?" Chris asks as the saleswoman prepares the invoice on a two-karat, princess-cut diamond in a platinum band.

"This is the only thing I'm sure of," I say.

"Hold the melodrama, Brody. I just want to know that you've thought this through."

"She makes me happy, Chris."

I can't remember a time I was really happy. Valerie gave me a chance to appreciate life because I wasn't alone anymore. I spent every free minute with her or talking to her or drawing for her. But I managed to take her for granted anyway with my constant melancholy.

It's not like Tiffany is a replacement, but when I'm around her I forget how much I've lost, how much I hate my life.

I couldn't explain this to Chris if I wanted to. I don't know how to explain that I need forever. Maybe I don't want to get married; I can't name a couple with a decent marriage. I just want Tiffany to stay.

The saleswoman comes back with the invoice, and I write a check for more than I spent on my new car. I hand it to her with pride. She doesn't know I didn't earn the money, that it's a consolation prize for being a cripple.

"Congratulations," she says as she hands me the

ring.

I'd gladly limp for the rest of my life if it kept Tiffany from leaving.

THIRTY-EIGHT

Tiffany looks away from her magazine long enough to eyeball me while I spring off the diving board and into her pool. "Don't hurt yourself," she teases from her lounge chair.

I graduated from stepping on balance balls and now I'm supposed to swim as often as possible to strengthen my leg. I swim a few laps, occasionally breaching the water to watch Tiffany flip through her magazine. Her skin is almost gold and the violet beach towel she's lying on contrasts it so perfectly that she practically glows.

I swim to the edge of the pool and hang my elbow over the edge.

"God damn, it's hot."

"You're hot," she says absently. She turns her page and says, "We should go on vacation. Like Florida maybe."

I let the idea drift past me. "Yeah."

"Yeah, you're stupid or yeah, we should go to Florida?" she asks, turning a page.

"Both."

I have carried the ring with me for two weeks, constantly worried about losing it, but more worried about missing the perfect chance to ask her. I want it to be special, obviously, but have had no legitimate ideas on making it special without making it a spectacle, which I also don't want. Florida, in its vague and lighthearted suggestion, is the answer.

"Let's go right now."

"What? Today?" She lifts her sunglasses off her face and lays the magazine down.

"Right now."

She sits up. "Right now?"

"Go pack," I say smiling.

She packs while I call Mom.

"I'm going to Florida," I say into the phone.

"What?" Mom asks.

"I said I'm leaving to Florida. I'll be back in a week."

"You really need to be getting ready for school."

"Yeah. When I get back," I say and hang up.

Tiffany is stuffing shirts into her red luggage when I grab her, lifting her up to hug her. My knee buckles and we both fall on the bed.

I carry her bags out and load them into the trunk.

"Are you sure you don't want to stop at your house?" Tiffany asks. The ring is in my glove box. I have an almost-full bottle of oxycodone, my toothbrush, a bag of weed, and a change of clothes in a bag on my back seat.

"I can get anything I need there." I kiss her and start the car.

THIRTY-NINE

Tiffany chooses a hotel on the beach that couldn't be any more expensive, but this secretly makes me giddy because I think it impresses her that I can pay for it. It makes her happy, at least, that I can feed her whims. Our room has a king bed with floor-to-ceiling windows and a view of the gulf. The view from the balcony is beautiful, even at night. The ocean beats itself against the shore but extends infinitely into the dark.

"What do you think of leaving the door open while we sleep so we can hear the ocean?" I ask Tiffany as she brushes her teeth.

"It's cold," she says. "We'll go out there tomorrow."

She's already ordered room service by the time I get up. We eat pancakes and eggs and bacon and fruit in bed. We have sex in the shower, then we find a spot on the sugar white beach where she lies down to sun herself.

Sitting next to Tiffany, surrounded by vacationers laughing and pretending to enjoy themselves, I realize how lonely I feel. I scoop a handful of sand from the beach and let the grains cascade through my fingertips. Every grain of sand is an ancient rock that was beaten to nothing by the constant force of the ocean. I brush it from my palms and walk waist deep into the water. The tide gently pushes against the shore, occasionally rising and crashing with enough force to push me toward humanity, only to pull me farther back to the vast and open nothing.

On land, Tiffany looks content to just lie in the sun. I trudge back to shore and yell, "Wanna race?"

"What about your leg?" she asks, barely looking up at me.

"Just get in here," I say.

She complains at first about how cold it is, but eases out toward me and we take off toward Mexico. The tide carries us faster than we swim, pushing me underwater with each wave. I stop swimming and paddle, looking back to see how far away the hotel seems. Tiffany keeps going, moving farther and farther out with each wave. I want to follow her, but I can't see through the water and I'm too far away from anything and I suddenly can't move.

I yell for her to come back. Everything moves farther away.

I wait for what feels like forever for her to notice that I'm not swimming with her anymore, that I'm constantly fighting the waves so I'm not carried farther out. I can't see past the algae-green skin of the water, and I can't hear anything but the waves.

Tiffany turns around and swims back to me, diving under the surface a few feet away. I feel something grab my leg and I instinctively yank away from it, kicking back toward shore.

She surfaces and says, "What's wrong?"

"I'm just really hungry all of a sudden," I lie.

We find a Mexican place, also with a view of the beach, and eat nachos. I can't talk the waiter into bringing me alcohol and this infuriates me, but Tiffany shoots me a look of detachment so I let it slide.

After lunch we have sex against the glass doors of

our balcony. Then we walk along the boardwalk and buy shirts and cheap bracelets from tourist shops. Tiffany decides she wants to go out on a boat, so I study for a minute and pass a test to get a boating license. Then she changes her mind and decides we would rather parasail. We parasail.

On the second day I give Tiffany my credit card and she leaves to go to the mall. I spend the day lying in the hotel room, alternately watching TV while smoking a joint and staring at the ring while smoking a joint.

Tiffany didn't mention that today is the one-year anniversary of Valerie's death, and neither did I.

On the morning of the last day, Tiffany pulls her bikini on and, with a wry smile, asks, "You ready?"

I've stressed myself out all week about the ring, waiting for it to be stolen when I leave it in the room or to lose it when I take it with me. As mortified as I am, I steel myself to asking her tonight.

"I'm going to run and get some food first," I say.

She shrugs and sets out to lie on the beach while I plod down the street to a liquor store. Walking and swimming has taken a toll on my leg, making it impossible to avoid limping.

A bum sits outside the liquor store and I weigh my chances of getting served against losing money on having the bum buy me alcohol. I decide I have better chances with the bum.

After I explain my order, I hold up a fifty and say, "So tell me again what you're getting."

"A bottle of nice champagne, man. I'm not an idiot," the bum says.

"What kind of champagne?" I drill him again.

"Nice. The nice kind, man," he says. "God, man, I didn't realize you were going to be so fascist about this."

I hand him the money. "There's fifty more for you when you come back with the champagne." He scuttles into the liquor store.

I wait impatiently for fifteen minutes until he reappears with a bottle of sparkling white wine. "No," I tell him. "This wasn't the arrangement. Go back. Get champagne."

"Ugh, man" is all he says before he retreats into the liquor store. I wait for half an hour while he's inside. I'm about to go in when he scuttles out, produces a bottle of champagne, and says, "It's the same shit, man. The same shit."

I pay him and walk to a deli across the street where I buy three sandwiches. He's gone when I come out, so I throw the extra sandwich away. In the hotel room I chill the champagne in a bucket of ice, very satisfied at seeing the project completed. Then I take the sandwiches to Tiffany and we eat them on the beach.

At dusk, we sit with our feet in the tide and watch the sun melt into the ocean. It's so beautiful it seems fake, like someone smeared orange and yellow acrylic paint across the sky. In the sunset, I kiss her and finger the ring in my pocket.

As the sun fades, I gather the courage to pull my heart from my chest. "Tiffany," I say, my inflection somber, "will you marry me?"

"Are you serious?" She rolls her body toward mine.

"Is that a yes or a no?" I ask as I slide the ring on her finger.

"You're serious!?" she squeals. "Why would you want to marry me?"

I kiss her, deep and slow. "I want to put you in a white dress and fuck you forever."

"Broderick, that is, by a wide margin, the sweetest

thing anyone has ever said." She stares at the ring, smiling, before she adds offhandedly, "But, you know, you'd need to do something about your scars if we ever want to have kids."

FORTY

I leaf through an old magazine in the dermatologist's waiting room, but I'm not really reading it, I'm just waiting for someone to drag me back for surgery.

Surgery for the scars I can't hide.

I wore a polo shirt to my college orientation – a weekend-long introduction to school before the semester started – and caught one of the counselors staring openly at the raised, plasticky scars all over my left arm. When she realized I was looking back at her, she looked at me with disgust and didn't acknowledge me for the rest of the weekend.

"I told you," Tiffany said when I complained about it. "You need to get those fixed."

"I don't want them fixed," I said and she looked at me like no one had ever said something so stupid.

My mom was the one who actually researched it. She jumped at the opportunity to "take care of that little problem." She found the dermatologist, called, and arranged the consultation.

"Broderick," a nurse says as she walks through the waiting room door. I make eye contact and she says, "Come on back."

"Now, Broderick," the doctor says, "I want to remind you not to set your expectations too high here. The laser will flatten the scars and reduce the redness, but the scars will still be visible."

The scars, he says, not *your* scars.

"If you want them completely gone, you're going to need to see a plastic surgeon."

The laser works, he told me before, by targeting the pigment cells in my skin. Deadening my skin. Killing it.

"When I start," he says, "it's going to feel like a constant bee sting, okay?"

I nod.

"I want you to let me know if the pain gets to be too uncomfortable at any time during the process. If you can't take it, if it becomes unbearable, just let me know and we'll take a break or schedule another session. We need to do at least four and it doesn't hurt to stretch them out."

"How long should it take?" I ask.

"For the scars we're treating, the amount of skin they cover, we're going to need to laser you a couple hundred times. A little less than an hour."

"I'll deal," I say.

"That's the spirit." He springs up and pats the medical chair, covered in its own roll of medical toilet paper. "Take your shirt off and get comfortable."

I peel my shirt off over my head and sit at the edge of the table. He puts on a pair of cheap looking red sunglasses and adjusts the laser.

I run my fingers over the scars and remember sitting in that parking lot, feeling like if I didn't cut the pressure was going to tear through my skin anyway. If suddenly every scar were filed down, scrubbed off my body, they'd still be on the inside.

"Lie back," he says. "It'll be over in no time."

As the laser heats up, before it burns the first skin cell to kill the pigment in my skin, I realize that I love my scars,

and that I will make more.

FORTY-ONE

"Do you speak English?" I ask the tan, Asian boy unpacking in my dorm room. I set my clothes on a twin mattress so old its edges curl in.

"Dude?" he snaps. "I'm from Chicago." He's my age, but he looks more youthful, cleaner, with black hair and tailored clothes.

"Broderick," I say, extending my hand with a smile that teeters dangerously on the border of sincere. My dress shirt hangs loose and unbuttoned, its sleeves rolled up above my elbows.

"Ken."

We shake.

"Are you always a dick?"

"Yeah," I say. I like him immediately.

The room feels the way I imagine a prison cell would feel if it had been made in the '60s – painted concrete with cheap ceiling tile. A single, vertical window slit into the concrete wall offers a decent view of the parking lot and then outward into the campus. Outside, waves of students unload boxes from their parents' cars and haul them toward their new home.

"So," I say, lying on the naked mattress.

"Yeah?" Ken folds his clothes and stacks them in a drawer.

"Where are your parents?" I ask.

"Like, why aren't they here? They didn't want me to come here. My dad's a doctor. He wanted me to be one, too." He finishes folding clothes and starts to unpack another bag. "My dad," he says, "thinks I owe him something anyway. I'm not giving him the satisfaction. So I took a full ride here, even though it isn't the best school that accepted me. I figure better to start now."

"Start what?"

"My own life."

My pants vibrate with a text message from Tiffany that says she's unpacked and needs my help hanging posters. The phone is a leash, disguised as a present that Mom gave me for going to college. I thought about leaving the plastic clamshell at my house, but decided to take it with me after Tiffany sent me a picture message of her naked breasts.

From the doorframe I half ask and half tell Ken, "Tiffany, my girlfriend – well, fiancée – we're going to find some dinner in about an hour if you want to come."

"Yeah, cool."

"I'll call the room when we're ready to go," I say, and then I wait at the elevator for what feels like forever. After six minutes of waiting, I walk down the seven flights of stairs, limping progressively worse with each floor, and make my way across campus to Tiff's dorm.

"So," Tiffany says as she claims a table, "someone invited me to a welcoming party when I was unpacking." We eat at a chain deli, which is fine but crowded. Ken and Tiffany seem to get along. I pile jalapeños on my sandwich until it's inedible.

"Guy or girl?" I ask flatly.

"What does it matter?" she answers.

"Yeah, a party is a party," Ken says through a

mouthful of food. "This town is tiny – what else is there to do?" They outvote me.

It isn't far from campus, so we walk. The party is a beacon, its thumping bass audible from five blocks away. The house itself is ancient, maybe as old as the campus, but it pulses and breathes with the life of two hundred students as they pour out of its doors and infest the yard, swarming around the kegs.

My leg burns from the walk over, so I down two Solo cups of beer before pouring my third and rejoining Tiffany to stand awkwardly behind her. She's showing some girls from high school her ring.

"Ooh. He has good taste," one of the girls says like I'm not there.

Another girl looks at me and says, "I heard about your accident. You have the worst summer luck."

"He has the devil's luck," Tiffany says. She leans into me and touches my shoulder. "Every time something bad happens to him something good happens, too."

I nod. Sip my drink. Something bad happened to Valerie last summer, not me. But I went to school with these girls for four years and don't know a single one of their names, so I don't bother explaining the difference.

Ken touches my shoulder and says, "They have the real stuff inside." I excuse myself and follow him through the crowd into the house. Ken and I wade through the drunks into a hallway hung with yellowing wallpaper. The wallpaper sags and has pulled off in sheets to reveal cracks in the foundation of the house.

In the living room we find a facsimile of a bar – an adult lemonade stand, really. Pool balls crack like gunshots under a neon Rolling Rock sign.

"I hear the guys who live here throw these parties to pay the rent," Ken says. I wonder if he wants me to know this or if he just wants to tell me. Maybe just talking is more important than the message.

I'm trying to listen to Ken but can't help overhear the guys behind me talking. "My brother was killed in a drive-by chainsawing," a stranger says, not talking to me. "It's dangerous in Maine."

A pool ball launches from the table and hits me in the arm. I pick it up from the floor and roll it in my fingers. A hoss of a boy covered in Greek lettering eyeballs me over his stubby, red nose. He holds his hand out, his face demanding. Something in his countenance reminds me of Saul, and I consider tearing the house down to bury him in it.

But Tiffany's outside, giggling with her friends.

I toss the ball back onto the table and buy a round of shots.

FORTY-TWO

After my geography class I go sit in the quad and read *Less Than Zero* while I wait for Tiffany.

"What's that all over your pants?" she asks when she finds me. She points at my crotch. I dog-ear my book and lift my shirt so she can see a perfectly copied map of Asia drawn onto my jeans in permanent marker.

"Political boundaries quiz," I say.

She frowns and says, "You're stupid." Then she takes my hand in hers.

"Aced it. Thanks for asking."

"You don't get to say you aced it when you're cheating."

"You never cheat?" I ask, smirking.

"Let's get high before lunch."

I nod, "Yeah, okay."

In the cafeteria I grab a chicken patty and some nachos, then find Ken and sit at his table, setting my book in an empty seat to save it.

Tiffany brings a new girl over. "Ken," she says, "this is my friend, Cynthia." Cynthia's mouth splits into a wide, gummy smile. They sit down and we eat.

"I think they'd make a cute couple," Tiffany says as we leave.

I shrug.

"You want to go with me to the library?"

I nod.

Outside the library I see a yellow flyer – open auditions for student-directed plays. I take it down and fold it into my pocket. When Tiffany and I declared majors, she knew she wanted political science. I read over the list and didn't see anything that was more interesting than anything else. I've been faking smiles since I can remember, so theatre seemed like an easy enough choice.

Tiffany and I get coffee at the library café and find a couch in front of a floor-to-ceiling window. She opens her laptop and I read *Less Than Zero* until she turns to me and says, "I can't imagine doing this without you." I smile and she runs her fingers through my hair. "I feel so good with you here next to me."

"Yeah?" I ask.

"It's like I brought a piece of home with me."

I kiss her and go back to my book.

"I need a book for class." She takes off her non-prescription glasses. "Will you go find it for me?"

"Write it down." I get up to find the librarian.

There is this attitude, almost tangible, like all of this is for us. In the library, surrounded by books and computers and scientific journals, I feel like I could grow. Do better. And I feel like I'm entitled to it.

"I need this book," I say, sliding Tiff's note to the librarian. "Where do I get it?"

"Google it," this asshole snaps at me like I'm the asshole. And I am, because I know better.

I walk back to the sofa where Tiffany is set against a bookshelf full of solid, heavy books in a library full of books no one knows how to find.

"I just Googled it," she says as I sit down. "Give me your credit card."

I dig it out of my wallet. She hugs me. I brush her hair out of her face and kiss her.

FORTY-THREE

I power through a lap in the pool at the gym with my weak, clumsy form. It's been months since rehab ended, but my knee burns and something inside it twitches, so I take another lap.

A girl passes me in her lane, like she has passed me on every lap I've swum. I stop and cling to the side of pool, watching as her arms raise and lower effortlessly, gracefully.

I push off, keeping my head underwater, looking side to side as I kick and pull myself along. I make it down about one-fourth of the lane before I surface for air. Ken stands by the edge of the pool in his sneakers. I plow through the water, splitting a path, and pull myself out to meet him.

"Want to grab a smoothie?" he asks.

"Sure," I shrug. "I was done anyway."

I towel off and skip showering, pulling my shirt on as we walk to the gym's juice bar.

"Why do you push yourself so hard in there?" he asks.

"What do you mean?"

"You looked like you were about to drown, dude."

"I guess that's why," I say and order a drink.

FORTY-FOUR

The auditions are this big thing where everyone's reading for every part in a whole slew of shitty one-act plays. I wait forever in the hall with people reading out loud to themselves like it isn't the single most annoying thing a human can do.

When I get called in, I stand in front of six people at a table, all of them looking at me to perform.

I read the lines. I don't know what I'm auditioning for.

I have no idea what I'm doing.

"Can you squawk like a bird?" this heavily pregnant woman asks.

I do it. I squawk like a bird. This is when I realize acting isn't for me.

"Okay," she says. "Great. Now show me your abs."

I get cast as a bird-monster.

I meet the rest of the cast in an empty classroom. The director, Maggie, wants me there to watch the rehearsal, even though I've only got one line – one word – so I watch as she sits sideways at her desk, her pregnant belly too big to fit, and tells the girls in the play what a good job they're doing.

The script is this terrible story about a girl who fucks a bird-monster. Only, it isn't about her fucking the bird-monster or meeting the bird-monster or even really about the bird-monster at all. It's about the girl after she fucks the bird-monster, and how she gets pregnant and is waiting to see if the baby is a bird-monster. Anyway, I think that's why she's waiting. The most dramatic scene in the whole play is when the girl's friend tries to talk her into getting an abortion.

The cast is small: three girls plus me. They're all pretty in a vacant, worthless way. One of the girls, Julia, could be a model if she didn't look so methed-out. I recognize her because she sometimes sits on a bench outside my dorm and never seems to be doing anything or waiting on anyone. She always seems out of place.

Ken, Tiffany, and Cynthia wait for me outside the library after practice. Ken offers me his flask and I wave it off.

"He's already tipsy," Cynthia says, giggling.

"Oh yeah," he says, nodding. "Pregame strategy. I'm on a stipend, you know."

"Smart," I say.

Tiffany laughs. "I've kind of forgotten what it's like to not be able to afford something."

"Rub it in!" Cynthia says, giggling again, maybe a little tipsy herself.

People here, they go home for the weekend – see their families, boyfriends, whatever. They live their lives and they're only here Monday through Thursday, so Thursday becomes the de facto Friday. The goal tonight is to go to every bar in town until we find one that will serve us and then get falling down drunk before Ken and Tiffany go home.

The bouncer doesn't even ID us at the first place, The Rotten Apple. He just shoos us away.

"Let's just go back," Cynthia says, discouraged.

"We'll find one," Tiffany says. She unbuttons her

coat, revealing a low-cut shirt, and we walk across the street to The Olive Pit. I try to bribe the bouncer, hand him a twenty with my ID. He looks at the bill, then back to me, and just says, "No." He's a foot shorter than me and looks like he'd roll down a hill if I pushed him over, but he hands my money back and looks at me like I'm the loser.

Tiffany pulls my arm and says, "Come on. Not worth it."

"God, it's fucking cold," Ken says to himself as we walk from bar to bar. He pulls a sip from a flask and puts it back in his vest pocket.

"What is that?" Cynthia asks, stopping to point at a neon sign in the alley between a Greek and an Italian restaurant: The Voodoo Lounge.

Tiffany shrugs. "Let's look."

A flight of concrete stairs leads us to a storm shelter of a basement. Windowless. Smoke so thick I can taste the ash. But there's no doorman. The bartender doesn't even ask for ID as I lean across the packed bar, waiting at least a full song from the Nirvana cover band before I can get his attention.

"Beer!" I yell over the crowd.

"What kind?"

"FOUR!" I yell, holding my fingers up for emphasis.

While I'm waiting at the bar, Ken gets on stage with the band.

"Oh fuck," I whisper under my breath as the singer looks him up and down.

I'm moving toward the stage when the singer smiles at Ken and asks, "What do you want to hear, boss?"

He holds the mic out to Ken. I pause, waiting for it to go bad. Ken takes the mic and stumbles back before he yells, "Who wants to see me-" pause, "rap battle-" he stands up straight, thrusts his hand toward the singer and yells, "him!"

Fucking Ken.

The bar goes crazy. The bartender pops the tabs on four beers and hands them to me like there's nothing weird about a drunk Asian kid challenging the band to a rap battle.

Ken goes first. I can barely hear what he's saying over how loud the music is but people keep cheering, egging it on. I maneuver through elbows and smoke back to Tiffany and Cynthia, who are watching, dumbfounded, as Ken rhymes over a karaoke version of "Sweet Home Alabama." Tiffany and Cynthia clap along and yell.

"I had no idea he could do that," Cynthia says as Ken passes the mic off.

I drink my beer and then Ken's.

The guy raps just as fluidly as Ken. When he finishes, the bar erupts in applause. Ken stumbles into the crowd and finds our table. We hang out for a few hours. Ken can't keep up with all the drinks people buy him.

FORTY-FIVE

Everyone leaves for the weekend. Ken goes. Tiffany goes home to visit her family.

I lie in my dorm room on my single bed, the mattress so thin I can feel the springs stabbing through it, and listen to The Killers.

My room is freezing.

On Ken's side of the room he's hung movie and music posters: *Fight Club* and The Beatles. Two weekends after school started, when everyone was settled, there was a big poster sale that filled the student center. I couldn't walk to the cafeteria or the bookstore without walking past posters of everything anyone could have cared about. Spider-Man to Britney Spears to *Scarface* to Weezer.

Two weeks must have been just enough time for the average student to feel trapped in his new prison cell of a dorm room. Two weeks of staring at painted concrete and they were all dropping $50 on posters to liven their rooms up.

Now it's the middle of October and I still haven't put up anything.

I look around my room, inventorying the things worth bringing from home, mostly just clothes and toiletries. I pull my shirt drawer out of the dresser Ken and I share, dig under my clothes and pull out the only special thing I brought: my box of X-Acto knives. I open it and rub my finger over the blades, then remember the promise I made to Tiffany and put the box back.

I walk downstairs to the lobby, twirling a cigarette in my fingers. The hall and stairwell are empty. The lobby attendant is reading a magazine as I pass him on my way outside. It's colder than I expected, but I sit on a bench by the entrance and take slow draws off my cigarette, letting the plumes of smoke roll over my face as I exhale.

With everyone gone, the campus feels desolate.

I flip my phone open to call Tiffany, but when I do I see the time and date on the display and realize that it's Valerie's birthday, so I light another cigarette instead.

FORTY-SIX

Death Cab for Cutie plays onstage, lasers and lights bouncing off the walls. I'm higher than usual, so the lights, the way they melt into the smog from the smoke machine, are glorious. They eclipse the band, the solemn tone of the breathy and foreboding music.

I don't even like Death Cab, but I let Tiffany talk me into buying her and her friends tickets. She sits next to me, so into the band it's like I'm not here. A few of her friends sit beside her, their faces dumb as they stare at the stage.

The band plays another song with the same vibe as the last three. I lean over to Tiffany, see her friend Luke leaning his head on her shoulder, and fight back a pang of anger before I whisper, "I'm going to the bathroom." She barely notices, nodding her head slightly in a way I imagine won't bother Luke.

In the bathroom I splash cold water against my face and examine it in the mirror, noticing how bad the purple circles under my eyes are. In the lobby I buy a hot dog and take it outside to sit in the cold and eat it.

The whole universe is inside, listening to the same song over and over, and I'm just waiting for it to end.

Tiff lets the car drift into the passing lane as she peels

the shrink wrap off a new Death Cab CD. A passing car honks and she yanks the wheel and pulls us back into the right lane.

"I'll do that," I say.

"I got it," she says, popping the CD in. I recline my seat and roll down the window as the stereo blares studio versions of the same songs I just wasted two hours on. She sets her hand on my leg and squeezes as she sings, which really pisses me off.

Behind us, her friends flash their brights. They speed up, pull beside us, and Luke and the girl in the passenger seat moon us. The car speeds in front of us and they laugh through the back windshield as Tiffany cracks up.

"I'm going to flash them," she squeals.

"Don't," I say.

"Stop pouting." She speeds past them, riding in oncoming traffic as she lifts her shirt.

"What are you doing?" I ask, sitting up. She passes them, still laughing.

"What do you mean?"

"Stop this." I lift my knee and brace my shin against the dashboard. She puts her hand on my leg, and I shake it off.

"What's wrong with you?"

"Let me drive."

"What? No." Her friends speed up to pass and she pulls over into their lane, blocking them.

"Fucking stop this," I say, and then, as though it was shaken free from someplace unknown, a balloon of loose and unwoven memories bursts open. Flecks of the car accident unravel: me, yelling, slamming my fist against the dashboard; her, speeding through stop signs and weaving through traffic; me, slamming the car door, walking away; her, following in the car, screaming at me to get back in.

I feel my features harden around my clenched

jaw. "Tiffany," I ask, my voice stern, "what were we fighting about before the accident?"

She looks over at me but doesn't speak.

Her friends pull into the right lane and they pass as I start to scream, repeating, "What were we fucking fighting about?"

"Stop yelling at me!" Her composure cracks. She looks over to her friends. "You've completely ruined this. You're so fucking embarrassing." The other car passes, pulls away.

She's silent for a long time before she starts to cry.

"What are you crying about?" I demand as I kill the radio.

"I don't want to talk about it." She turns the radio back on.

"What happened before we got in the wreck?" My voice goes cold as I ask. She drives, both hands wrapped tightly on the wheel, eyes welled up with tears.

She pulls up on campus and speeds toward my dorm.

"I'm not-" I growl, but catch myself and steady my voice. "I'm not getting out of this car until you tell me what fucking happened."

She pulls in front of my dorm.

"Get out." She stares ahead.

Her friends pull up behind her and honk. I sit planted in her car and say, "I'm not leaving this car until you tell me."

Her friends keep honking to the tune of "Jingle Bells."

"Get out," she says before she starts to cry again. "Just get out."

I look at her for a long time, trying to answer the question myself, before I climb out of the car. She speeds off before I can slam the door. Her friend's car lingers for a second before following.

I watch them go, watch their taillights fade, before I go inside and upstairs to my room where I keep my X-Acto knives.

FORTY-SEVEN

I don't see Tiffany for almost a week. She doesn't come to the cafeteria or answer her phone, so I walk to her dorm after her last class to wait outside the back entrance, hoping to run into her.

Knowing there's something I don't know has to be worse than whatever it is.

I wait for what feels like hours before the girl from the play, Julia, steps out from the back door. She leans against the wall and looks at me vacantly as she pulls a pack of cigarettes from her purse.

"Brody, right?" she asks.

I nod.

I bum a cigarette off her and light them both with a match from a Voodoo Lounge matchbook.

"I love that place," she says. "One time I saw this Asian guy, completely wasted, stumble on stage and rap."

"That's hilarious." I punctuate my sentence with an unnecessarily long drag, holding the smoke in my mouth.

"Maybe I'll see you there some time," she says.

I smile and say, "Maybe."

"See you at rehearsals," she says and walks away without looking back. As she clears the street toward my dorm, I run my hand up the arm of my jacket and rub the fresh scars on my forearm.

I've almost given up on catching Tiffany when a car pulls up to the door, blinding me with its headlights. I can't see the driver, but Tiffany gets out of the car with one of the girls who went with us to the concert.

Her face sours when she sees me, mid-laugh. Like seeing me reminded her that she was miserable. Her friend sees me and her face twists into an equally sour expression.

"You're going to play this like I did something to you?" I say as they walk past me without acknowledging me. Her friend turns to scowl at me and I add, "Fuck you. The only experience you've ever had with me was me buying you shit so keep your opinion to yourself."

"Fuck you," she says, awestruck.

"Just leave, Brody," Tiffany says as she slides her key card and opens the back door. I grab it before it closes and follow them up the stairs. She plods ahead of me like I'm not there so I grab Tiffany's wrist and say, "I need to talk to you."

She yanks her hand from mine and we have a conversation in sneers and rolled eyes before she dismisses her friend, saying, "I'll see you later."

"Are you sure?" she asks.

Tiffany nods.

I follow her in silence to her room where I sit on her bed and wait for her to talk. In the few days since I've been in her room she has redecorated her door, bought new bedding, and changed most of her posters. Also, I don't see the picture we took at the beach after I asked her to marry me, which was in a frame by her bed.

She stares at me for a long time. Being so close to her body, to her skin, is excruciating.

"I don't understand what's happening," I say.

She runs her fingers through my hair, catching

them on a knot. "When was the last time you took a shower?" she asks gently. I pull my head away and glare at her, realizing that I haven't since I cut myself the night of the concert.

I take her hand from my face. "Tell me what happened."

"After what happened last time I told you, I don't want to." She crosses her arms across her chest. She takes a step back and starts crying.

"You cheated on me," I say.

"Have you known this whole time?" she asks.

"No." I hunch forward. "But what else could it be?" She inches toward me. "Who was it?"

"I'm not talking about it, not after what happened last time."

"You owe me the truth," I say, eyes on the floor. "I need to know."

"That's what you said last time. You said you would forgive me if I told you. And then you jumped out of the car downtown when I was stopped at a red light." She sniffles and starts to cry. "I begged you to get back in the car and then the accident happened. I've known we were done since."

"Then why have you dragged it out for so long? Why did you let me ask you to marry me? Why the fuck did you say yes?"

"When I saw you in the hospital after the accident, I knew I loved you and it broke my heart." Her tears come in sheets as she talks through her sobbing. "I thought – oh God, I don't know what I thought. I've just been waiting for this since."

"Who was it?" I ask again.

She cries harder, which makes me want to put my fist through a window. She should be pledging to fix it. She should be begging for me to forgive her. Instead it's about her. She fucks up and wants pity for it.

"I think I hate you." I regret the words before I say them, but I can't stop them from coming out.

Her face turns solemn as she cries harder. "You need to leave."

"What?"

"Get out. We're done."

"You're telling me we're done? Fuck you! You can't break up with me! You're the fucking cheater!"

"Just leave, Broderick."

"Tiffany," I start to cry. "Don't do this."

"What do you want me to do?"

"Fix it."

"I can't. You can't undo something like that."

"You haven't even fucking tried!" I yell, my whole body clenching.

She opens the door and stands by it impatiently. "Please, just go."

"Tiff," I choke. "Don't leave me."

I start to sob, which makes her cry harder. She wants to hug me, I can see it, but she doesn't budge.

"Never mind," she says. "Stay here as long as you need to. Lock the door when you leave." She walks through the doorway and says, "I'll always love you."

"Wait," I say.

She hesitates in the doorframe.

"Give me the ring."

"You don't need it," she says.

"Neither do you, you fucking cheater."

She slips the ring from her finger and hands it to me, then lets the door slam behind her as she leaves.

I lie on her bed for a long time trying to catch my breath before I rifle through her drawers looking for the picture of us at the beach. I can't find it, but I do find a note to her from some fuck named Wayne. I take the note and the ring and leave.

FORTY-EIGHT

I drag myself across the street to my dorm, look up at the seven-story building, and then turn into the parking lot to find my car. I pull a wad of tickets from under my windshield wiper and get in before I throw them out the window.

Under the languid cast of my car's dome light I read the note:

Tiffany,
I know that there is no way you have ever felt like I do now, because you're so beautiful and everyone likes you immediately and no one would ever deny you. But I look at you and it makes me feel worthless because I know I could never be good enough for you. I just want you to know that, even though you don't like me. I think you're an amazing person and anyone would be lucky to have you in their life, even for a minute. I hope that maybe you could possibly one day look at me and think that, that you would be happy to have me in your life. But I know you probably won't.
I can't just be your friend. Because I love you.

Sincerely,
- Wayne

FORTY-NINE

The next day I score some pot and take a drive down a long farm road to smoke it. I light a joint and drive until it's spent, then I toss the roach out the window and keep driving. The overcast sky blankets everything: houses, a few forsaken businesses, and field after field of grazing cows.

I light another joint. Desolate farmhouses pepper the road like mile marker signs. A small church appears in the distance. I decide to stop there to turn around.

I pull into the church before I realize that it sits in front of a football field-sized graveyard. I kill my engine and I walk through the necropolis, stepping over lumps of dried leaves that crunch like small bones and running my fingers over decaying headstones that crumble to the touch.

A breeze whistles through so I pull my hood on and light another joint, cupping my hands over the lighter when the wind puts the flame out.

Some of the stones have two names – for a husband and wife who are buried together. I take a knee in front of a husband-wife combo stone. Pearl was born in 1903, Chauncey in 1901. They were married in 1921. Chauncey died in 1924, but Pearl lived well into her fifties.

I sigh, then choke a little on the weed and have a

coughing fit.

They only had three years.

If I had a choice, I'm not sure if I'd want to be married to Valerie or Tiffany, or even at all. I wonder, though, if Pearl had any kind of life after 1924; if she remarried or ever even loved someone else; if that love tarnished her first; if she regretted any of it.

I wonder if my parents each loved someone more intensely than each other before they got married. If everyone is doomed to remember the one who got away.

I wonder if any of these headstones, the ones with both names, were made after their lovers committed suicide.

I start to cry.

Valerie told me she was a virgin when we started dating, and she never changed her story. But her friends all made a point to tell me that she'd had sex with her previous boyfriend. She and I fought about it for months. I couldn't let it go. I said nasty things to her every time I thought about it. When we started fighting it was about that, but then it was about nothing. I fought with her almost every time I saw her, and when I couldn't do it anymore I broke up with her.

The next day she was dead.

I light another joint, but just keep crying. I call Tiffany to tell her I'm sorry, but she doesn't answer so I assume she's with Wayne and leave her a nasty message about how much I hate her.

FIFTY

I call Tiffany every few hours for about a week. I try not to, but I can't stop myself from dialing, listening to the ring, waiting through to the dial tone. It's like there's a permanent crack in my focus. If I find myself involved in something, paying attention, all it takes is a break in concentration and I have to stop and call her.

She's a cheater, but in the few weeks we've been separated I've done almost everything alone. I don't want to be with her, but I don't want her gone.

"Dial star, six, seven," Ken says, lying in bed watching a courtroom drama.

"Mute that," I say. He turns the TV off. I block the number and call him. When it rings he tosses me his phone so I can see that my information shows up as 'unavailable.'

I redial Tiffany with my number blocked and she picks up on the first ring.

"Hello?"

I wait, listening to her breathe.

"Hello?"

Suddenly I realize that I don't have anything to say.

"Brody, I know this is you. Don't be a creep."

I slam the phone shut as fast as I can.

"Did it work?" Ken asks. I shake my head and toss the phone on my desk. I can't tell if he cares or if he's just sick of seeing me pout. "She'll come around, man. Just give her some time. Let's get some food." He thinks for a second then adds, "Things always work out for the best."

I can't bring myself to tell him that's not true. He doesn't know about Valerie, or about how people said that to me for months after she died. "Things always work out for the best." Things worked out very poorly for her.

"Order a pizza," he says, sitting up.

I call out for delivery. "How many toppings can I get on a single pizza?" I ask.

"You can get eight toppings on a large," the operator answers.

"Give me a large pizza. With eight sausage toppings." Ken looks at me and sighs. "And whatever fairy pizza you have, too."

"I don't understand, sir."

"Like, garden veggie or some shit."

"Okay," he says. "One sausage with extra sausage, and one garden-veggie-or-some-shit fairy-pizza. Can I get your address?"

When I meet the delivery guy in the dorm lobby, Julia is sitting on her bench in the rain. Soaked. I pay the driver and yell out to her from the door, "What's wrong with you?"

She smirks like it's a challenge. I sigh and walk out toward her, holding the pizza boxes at my hip.

"Want some pizza?"

"Sure," she says through a smile.

I introduce Ken to Julia. "She's in that play." Ken, always cordial, gets her a towel. Julia sits on my bed and we eat pizza and stare at each other. She brings each bite to her mouth with tiny flutters of grace and I can't help but notice how loud I'm chewing.

"Do you have anything to drink?" Julia asks, but before I answer I feel my pocket vibrating. Without thinking I snap it open. When I see Tiffany's name on the caller ID I break into a cold sweat.

"You need to answer that?" she asks as the phone buzzes in my hand.

"No," I lie, panicked.

"Is it her?" Ken asks.

"Who?" Julia locks her huge brown eyes with mine.

"No one," I say, closing the phone.

"You can answer it," Julia says, setting her half-eaten slice of pizza back in the box.

"It's okay," I say again.

"Well," she says, standing up, "I should really go anyway."

"See you later," Ken says.

I walk her to the elevator in silence and wait for it to come to my floor. When it does, she steps on and smiles at me, a bittersweet smile that feels like a frown.

I wait for the doors to close before I call Tiffany back. She doesn't answer on the first ring so I call her again as I walk to the stairs. When I get her voicemail I hurry down the stairs and call her room.

Busy signal.

I run through the rain to Tiff's dorm. When I get there she still hasn't answered her phone and the light in her room is out. I pace around her parking lot, calling her back over and over for almost an hour before I give up and go home.

FIFTY-ONE

In the pitch-black room the spotlight shifts to me, sitting shirtless on the floor in bird makeup, and I look longingly to the actress who portrays the girl who falls in love with the bird-monster and shout, "Squawk!"

Squawk: my single line in the entire play.

I'm on stage for all of six minutes, but it's long enough to see Tiffany when her cell phone lights up and bathes her face in its pale glow.

I'm on stage for six minutes, and she can't wait to answer her fucking text message.

The lights fade and stagehands rush to change the scene from a bird-monster's cave to a suburban family kitchen where the girl-who-fucks-the-bird-monster will get a firm lecture about consequences.

It turns out you can't love anyone without paying for it.

At curtain call, I walk back out with the cast. I'm still wearing my costume: black tights, fake bird wings, leather gauntlets to cover the faded scars on my forearms, a Tengu mask, and full makeup. The cast takes a bow. The director takes a bow. The audience stands up and walks onto the stage to shake hands with everyone.

While everyone is congratulating each other, Tiffany and her friends make for the door. I start off the stage and the director grabs my arm. "Good job tonight," she says, and I nod. "Where are you off to? Not going to help clean up?"

"Just give me a minute."

I ditch my mask and wings before I grab my hoodie and maneuver through the audience into the hall. I'm too late though, so I jog down the stairs and outside. I circle the building but don't see her, so I run through the quad toward the dorms where I find her crossing the street.

"Tiffany!" I shout.

She stops and motions to her friends that she'll catch up.

"Thanks for coming," I say as I clear the street.

"I wouldn't have missed it."

"I'm sorry it sucked."

"I just wish you were in it more is all." She brings the tips of her fingers gently to my face. "I like your makeup."

"Well," I say reaching to touch her wrist. For a single second the world is okay and nothing happened. For a single second she and I are the only people on Earth.

"Well," she says as she pulls her hand away. "I've got to go." She hesitates for a second, then turns to walk away. I follow beside her.

"That's it?"

"What else do you want?" she asks. I can sense her closing up.

"You didn't come to apologize?"

"Brody," she says weakly, then turns away.

"Right," I say. "You can't fix it so you're not even going to fucking try."

She looks at me sincerely and starts to cry.

"Why couldn't Wayne make it?"

Her tears stop abruptly. "What?"

"Your friend. Wayne. Why didn't he come?"

"I can't fucking believe you."

"You can't believe what? That I know about it?"

"I can't believe that you haven't seen me in weeks and you have me crying in the fucking street. You know what, I can believe it. You're such an asshole. Who even told you about him?"

"So, I'm right then? He's your boyfriend?"

"I'm done with this shit. I don't have to put up with this."

"That's a soft yes, then?" The gravel in my tone scares me. "It didn't take you a whole fucking month to find a new boyfriend? Were you fucking him before we broke up too?"

"Fuck this, Brody. Don't follow me. Just leave me alone." She starts off again down the street. I hold my trembling palms to my temple. I can't let her go; I don't want her to stay. I punch the brick wall of the building beside us and release a low, guttural growl.

"Will you calm the fuck down?" she asks, her eyes tight.

"I...I just..." I can't tell her. I don't even know.

"God, you're pathetic. You are so fucking selfish you can't act like a human long enough to say hi to me." She turns around and walks off in a half run, then turns around and yells, "And stop fucking calling me!"

I wait until she turns the corner and punch the brick again. Tears well up in my eyes, but people are starting to leave the theatre so I walk home as fast as I can.

"Did you break a leg?" Ken asks when I get back to my room. I was hoping he wouldn't be in here.

"No. But maybe I stepped on a nail."

"I have no idea what we're talking about anymore," he says.

"I don't ever know," I say, looking into the mirror

above my sink.

"Did the play go well?" he tries again.

I run the sink and try to scrub the makeup off my face.

"I don't even know. I didn't stay after. I squawked. So what else could they ask of me?" I say, still scrubbing.

"You'll get a bigger part next time, Brody." In the mirror I see Ken go back to studying. His books lie stacked up on his bed like he's been reading out of all of them. It feels like he's always working toward something.

Most of the makeup washes off my face, but black smears cling to my skin like raccoon eyes where the Tengu mask wouldn't cover. There's a cast party at this theatre major Davis's house to celebrate the student plays, and, staring into the mirror at my artificial black eyes, I decide there's probably no better place to self-destruct tonight.

"Good show, man," Davis says when I get to his house. I make a note to never accept praise from him based on how loosely he throws it around. The house is full of people I've seen before but don't know, and they're all two drinks in by the time I get there.

Another freshman – Billy, I think – jumps on me and screams, "SQUAWK!" I hold his weight for a second before my bad knee buckles and we both tumble to the floor, his beer soaking my hoodie.

"Fucking..." I stand up, shoving him off me.

"God dammit," Davis says.

"Oh, shit. Sorry, bro," Billy says, looking first at Davis and then at me. I peel my soaked hoodie off and lay it over a chair.

"Are you high, kid?" Davis asks, peeved.

"Shit," Billy slurs.

"Don't worry about it. Just get me a beer," I say.

He salutes me and disappears. "So, hey," I ask Davis, "did Julia come?"

"Julia?" he asks himself. "Hardbody?"

"I don't know. She was in the play with me. The mom."

"Oh shit, yeah. She's on the porch." He nods toward a back door.

My shadow obscures the porch light as I stand over Julia, who sits smoking cigarettes around a table with the other girls from the play, her hair effortlessly disheveled.

"Can I bum one of those?" I ask. She hands me the cigarette out of her mouth and her eyes linger on me in a vacuous way. "Um, thanks," I mutter, my confidence punctured. Billy finds me, a beer in each hand, and I take them both before waving him off and retreating to the bottom steps of the porch.

The cigarette turns to ash as I chug the first beer. I suck the second one down in long, slow gulps and dump the cigarette in the bottle. Leaning back against the steps, I watch a full moon decompose and melt into a wave of opaque clouds.

Soft steps creep behind me and I look back to see Julia walking down the stairs alone. "You mind some company?" she asks, taking a seat on the step above mine. We both lie back against the stairs, my shoulder against her stomach, with our arms outstretched as we gaze at the stars. "They really put this in perspective," she says. Her voice sounds soft and faded like she's stoned.

She lights another cigarette.

"I don't know." I regret saying it. I wish I said something more interesting or nothing at all. I reach back with two fingers and pluck the cigarette from her mouth, take a drag, and replace it.

"I can't figure you out. What are you so hung up on?" Julia asks.

I rest my eyes on hers. She breaks my gaze, leans forward, and touches her lips to mine softly, not pushing far enough to actually kiss me. Her lips linger on mine.

"I need another beer," I say as I stand and take her hand gently in mine to lead her through the house. She plants on the couch. I get some beer and some mostly liquid Jell-O shots some idiot left under the stove light.

I want so hard to play it cool with her, but I cave and tell her about Tiffany. She listens and nods as I talk about the last few weeks. "Do you think she's a bad person?" Julia asks, catching me off guard.

"No." I tip my beer and kill it. "I don't think people are good or bad or black or white. People fuck up. Everyone is gray."

She sets her beer on the floor and climbs into my lap. "That's not true. You're black. And white. You're both, but not gray."

"What makes you say that?"

"I know because I'm black and white. Sometimes both at the same time. But never gray." She straddles me, her fingers gliding along my lips. "I knew you were like me as soon as I met you." She touches her lips to mine, softly at first, then deep.

When she kisses me, I feel wanted, like I matter. I run my fingers through her hair and kiss her back.

She curls up against me, her breath hot on the nape of my neck, and says, "You kiss like a girl."

FIFTY-TWO

I go out of my way to avoid Julia after the party. I'm not grounded on technicality, but I feel like I did something wrong.

I go to world geography, but I can't focus. I usually like listening in that class, but today I just end up drawing during the lecture while waiting for the class to end. I sketch for about an hour before I think about Tiffany. Then I check my watch and realize I've been in class for six minutes.

I collect my books and stand up to leave. As I walk toward the back of the room the professor calls out to me, "Do you have somewhere more important to be, Broderick?"

I look back and shake my head, no.

He nods his head at me in disappointment. I leave.

I call her on the walk to my dorm, but she doesn't answer. I'm so sick of her answering machine so I wait until I get home to call her again. There, I drop my bag and keys and sit against my desk. I call her cell with my cell and while it's still ringing I use my landline to call hers.

"Hello?" she answers.

"Tiffany?"

She's silent. I can almost feel her scowl at me.

"Listen, um." I sigh. "I just called because I felt

bad about the other night, and—"

"Brody." She cuts me off.

"I'd really just like to talk to you."

"It's not a good time."

I don't have time to respond before I hear a man's voice ask, "Who is that?"

"Is he over there right now?" I bark into the phone. She hangs up before I finish my sentence. I immediately start toward my car, my nerves smoldering, biological fuses for my spontaneous combustion. I need to catch her. I need to know.

My first step outside is in full sprint. I bound through the courtyard and into the parking lot. There is nothing elegant about my free running, no hint of style.

I'm running through the pain in my knee. I'm running because I can't not run.

I get in my car and race toward her dorm, parking far enough back on the street that I can see through her window, if only a glimpse. I get out of my car, pace in circles as I call her again.

People assume that when someone is out of control he's also unaware of it. I know I'm stalking. I know it's harassment as I call her and she doesn't answer so I call her again and again until I watch her take the phone off the hook and look out the window.

She looks right at me and I imagine that I can see some kind of sadness in her. For a second I wonder if I'm wrong. Then he sets his hand on her shoulder. My instinct is spot on. He's there: some fat, blonde, ruddy-faced fuck.

She closes the blinds.

And turns off the light.

I throw myself in my car, slamming the door, and break down, bashing my fist into the steering wheel, punching it over and over, until I collapse into it and start to bawl.

I sit seething, teeth clenched, my eyes like Armageddon. My breaths are short and panicky. I roll my pant leg up and fixate on her window as I use my pocketknife to tear deep into my calf.

I cut more furiously than I ever have before. Each cut spills more and more blood, spraying it on my seat, covering my hand. My leg is bleeding so bad that I can't see where I'm cutting. I drown myself in the pain, cutting until I can breathe steady, and then I close my knife and drop it against the center console.

I roll my pants back down and blood spreads through the fabric, plastering it to my leg.

I grip the wheel and breathe in. Breathe out. Drive away.

I drive aimlessly through town until I spot a pawn shop advertising guns. Blood has soaked through my sock completely so each step squishes through the wet, congealing slime. I make my way through the store in a lucid wandering until I stop at the firearms display. I lean against the unmanned counter and consider how easy it would be to kill Wayne. Or myself.

"Sir?" A young pawn broker stares at me, but keeps his distance. "Sir, can I help you find something?"

"No." I slap on my best Saturday-afternoon-barbecue smile. "Thanks, but I'm just looking."

"Um, do you realize you're bleeding?" He motions to my leg. "It looks really bad."

I look down at my leg. My pants are drenched and blood has soaked through my shoes. I look back to him and feign shock.

"Oh, well shit. I am."

"I think you should go to a hospital."

I take a deep breath before I drop my smile and say, "Did you know that when you bleed to death it isn't so much the blood loss that kills you? You die because you can't get the oxygen your cells need. It's serene, like drowning."

He looks at me like I'm deranged. "I'm going to call you an ambulance."

I pat his shoulder in affirmation as I say, "It's alright, man. I'll make it." I can feel him eyeballing me as I walk out of the store, a circus freak show act leaving bloody shoeprints. Each print has PUMA stamped in my blood, a new wave of morbid horror marketing.

And as I leave the store, my phone buzzes with a text message from Tiffany that reads: *I love you. Call me.*

FIFTY-THREE

Against my better judgment, I drag myself to meet Tiffany at the library café. When we order, she makes a point of paying for my drink. I raise my hand to stop her, but she says, "You always pay," and the cashier takes her money.

We find a table and sit across from each other.

"What do you want?" I ask, stone-faced.

She takes a sip of her coffee, stalling. I try to take a sip of mine, but it's too hot so I just pretend to drink it as I stare at her. "I think we made a mistake breaking up," she says.

"You made a mistake, you mean."

"Maybe I handled it wrong." She shifts in her seat and looks out the window. Everyone seems to be going somewhere, most of them done up in jackets and winter clothes. With finals coming up, campus is a little more solemn. "If you want to try again, I want to try again."

"I don't want to be with you."

"If you didn't want to be with me you'd stop calling and hanging out outside my window." I take the first sip of my coffee. It's still too hot, but I drink it anyway, remembering all the nights she called me just to see how I was, the times she took me in, saved me over and over.

She's the only one who knows what I really went

through.

"What about Wayne? What's he going to think about this?"

"God, Brody. This was a mistake." She stands up to leave and I grab her wrist.

"Wait," I say. "Don't go." She stops and stands by the table, glaring at me.

"You need to figure out what you want," she says. "If you want to be together you have to drop it. Wayne is just a friend I met in Math." The note I found in her dorm was so rambling and pathetic that I consider she might be telling me the truth. "But you have to forgive me for this to work," she says. "It's on you now. Do you think you can?"

"I don't know," I say, finally releasing her hand to rest my head on my palms.

"Well," she says, sitting back down, "why don't you take a few weeks. Let's see each other for Christmas. Things have just been so crazy lately. We just need to process this. We need time."

"Don't tell me what I need," I say in a low growl. "You can't have it both ways."

She stands up again. "Make up your mind," she says. "I'm leaving."

I press my palms into my temples, staring at the table. "Fine," I say, standing up. "I'll see you at Christmas."

She steps toward me and wraps her hands around my neck. "Good. This is going to be good for us." I lean into her, my forehead on hers, and sigh. "When can I come pick up the ring?"

I reel back out of her grip. I stare at her with as much contempt as I can muster, then trash my coffee and leave.

FIFTY-FOUR

The cold turns bitter before I take my geography final. It asks me to identify a lot of the countries that I did in the quizzes, but I haven't drawn a map of the world on my crotch, so I take my best shot and walk back to the dorm.

There's something about December that makes the weather feel a lot more like loneliness.

Ken's still out when I get back. He probably collapsed from lack of sleep, the way he's been studying. I throw some clothes in my bag and take my rolled joints, then I write "Merry Christmas" on a pretty substantial bag of loose pot and leave it on Ken's bed.

Julia is walking into the dorm as I walk out, so I stop and light a cigarette.

"Going home?" she asks.

I nod. "You?"

"Arizona's a long way away." She shifts her weight to lean on the door and motions toward my cigarettes. I give her one, standing close to block the wind as I light it.

"Sorry."

"I'm not." She takes a drag, then adds, "You should call me over the break if you get lonely."

"Maybe," I say as I pick up my bag. "Phone works both ways."

"Happy holidays," she says, standing up straight.

"Yeah," I turn to leave, but remember the joints in my pocket and hand her a few. "'Tis the season."

She smiles, her eyes soft and sincere, so I smile as I walk out to my car.

Mom hugs me when I come through the door and kisses my forehead.

"I missed you. You should visit more often," she says. "Do you want something to eat?"

I shake my head. My father comes in from outside and says, "I need your help splitting logs for the woodpile," which I think means he missed me too.

I set my bag down in my room. School is only a few hours away and I've only been gone for a few months, but my parents' house feels foreign, like I haven't been back in years.

FIFTY-FIVE

During my parents' first fight of the holiday – about whether they stored the decorative reindeer in the basement or the attic – I decide to get out of the house.

I go to the bookstore and order my coffee like Tiffany – too sweet with fake sugar syrups – and sit in the aisle between bookshelves to read graphic novels. When I finish every half-interesting-looking comic, I pick up *Moby Dick* and try to read it. I can't focus past the first few pages so I leave and drive by Tiffany's house just to see if she's home. She isn't, so I run my car through a car wash seven times and then go see a movie.

I call Nolan to hang out, but he's working nights at his new job, so I spend the rest of the week by myself. I call Tiffany a few times, but hang up on the first ring.

She's right – it won't work if I can't forgive her. If I could let it go, we'd settle back in. We'd go out to dinner and I'd buy her whatever she wanted and I'd know she was there.

Chris calls me when he gets back from school.

"Brody!" he says, his voice singsong. "How'd your semester go?"

I'm a little high, and I haven't talked to him in so

long that he catches me off guard. "Good. Good. Really great," I lie.

"It's been a long time. Would you want to hang out, catch up?"

"Well, yeah," I say, desperate to get out of the house. "I need to go Christmas shopping. You want to do that with me?"

"We can give it the old college try," he says.

We pick the worst possible time to go to the mall: Friday, a few hours before it closes. The stores are so congested that I feel like I'm going to have an anxiety attack every time someone looks in my direction.

Chris rambles about going to Yale. I'm happy for him, but it's mostly obnoxious. He mentions his major, Pre-Law, three times, even though he knows I know this already, but I have to keep up, nodding and saying "yeah" and "cool" and "that sounds nice" to seem interested.

"So, theatre. What can you do with that when you graduate?" he asks, flipping through a rack of sweaters.

"I was thinking about being a doctor or an architect or maybe a cosmonaut. Theatre isn't nearly as limiting as, wait, what's your degree again?" I flip through the same rack of sweaters.

"Pre-Law."

We stop in nearly every shop so I can find presents for Tiffany. I buy lingerie and dresses and chocolate – anything that looks expensive.

"So, why are you buying her so much shit if you broke up?"

"We're supposed to get back together on Christmas."

"That sounds super healthy," he says. "So, you're trying to buy her love back?"

"She's so distant now. We aren't together, sure. Yeah, I get how it looks. But, like," I sigh, "I don't know how to operate without her. Part of me hates her for cheating and part of me really needs her."

We walk into a clothing store. "People don't change. Neither of you are going to be different people even if you want it to work. She cheated on you, Brody. All the things you like about her, sure those are there, but she doesn't respect you or she wouldn't have done that."

"You don't know what you're talking about."

He looks at me and frowns. We walk in silence for a while until we pass a candy store and he says, "You remember when we were little and my parents would bring us here?"

"And we'd get bags full of gummy sharks and octopuses and shit like that? I remember you spending your week's worth of lunch money on it." We go through the store, filling oversized candy bags with the entire gummy animal kingdom. When we were twelve we'd eat gummy creatures until we wanted to vomit. Then we'd lie on his basement floor and play Sega Genesis.

"I remember these being a lot better," I say, biting into a gummy sea turtle.

"How did we eat so many of these?" He dumps his bag in a garbage bin as we pass it. I do the same, but save one great white gummy shark because I know I'll appreciate it later.

We leave the mall and walk out into the backdrop of falling snow, stepping around puddles of gray sludge to get to Chris's car.

"Hey, I know you don't want to hear this," Chris says as we dump the bags in his trunk, "but sometimes things just don't work out. I can kind of understand why you want it to so bad. I mean, things with Valerie couldn't have ended any worse than they did." This strikes a nerve. I climb into the passenger seat and wait for him, hoping he'll shut up. He gets in and starts the car, but doesn't take a breath. "And I still don't think that was your fault. I really don't. Well," he pauses before inching his way through the parking lot. "I applaud your indomitable nature, but sometimes things just don't work out. You can't make someone love you."

"Why do you say she doesn't love me?"

"Chill out. I'm not saying that. Is that all you heard me say just now? I'm saying that you shouldn't hold it against yourself if this relationship doesn't work out. That's all."

"Yeah." I deflate. A group of people waits at a bus stop. A bus passes without picking them up.

"Anyway, what do you want to get for dinner? Mexican? Italian? Chinese?" He says this like the conversation's over.

"I don't care," I say, realizing that our friendship is over.

FIFTY-SIX

My phone rings while I'm getting dressed to go eat with Mom. I rush to answer it, hoping it's Tiffany, but it's Julia.

"How's your break going?" she asks.

"I've never been more bored in my life. You?" I pull my pants off the floor and sit on my bed. As I pull them on, I notice how cleanly my leg has healed.

"I went on a cruise," Julia says.

I run my finger over the scars from the wreck, clean and slick like melted plastic. They almost look normal compared to the self-inflicted ones on my other leg, which stay purple and numb in the cold.

"Cool."

"Are you busy?" she asks.

"I'm actually on my way out the door," I say.

"Oh."

"Talk to you later," I say, and as I'm shutting the clamshell phone I hear her saying my name like she had something else to say.

After eating with mom, I drive by Tiffany's house. Her car isn't there, so I go by Puck's to pick up drugs.

Puck's house looks like an unaccomplished dump; his gutters have a small forest of dead trees growing up through the snow and leaves, the yard is littered with soda cans and debris, and patches of vinyl siding threaten to fall off in the yard.

I park across the street and text him: *P. I'm making sushi. Do you have any sea-Weed?*

I recline my seat to wait for his text, but he calls me instead. "Who is this?"

"Brody."

"Brody who?"

"How many people do you know named Brody?"

He pauses. "None. Who is this?"

"I'm a little hurt."

"What's all this about sushi?"

"I meant, like, do you have any drugs?"

"Shit, dude. Don't say that on the phone. You never know who might be listening, man."

"That's why I used a euphemism, Puck."

"What the fuck are you talking about?"

"Never mind. I'm across the street. I'll be at your door in a second."

I walk over and ring his doorbell. He answers wearing a bathrobe. "Well, shit, man, why didn't you just say it was you?"

"I did," I say.

He laughs. "Sit down, man. *Mi casa, su casa.*"

I sink into his sticky, pleather couch. His television, set up on a cardboard box, is playing *Finding Nemo*. "What can I do you for, man?"

"I need something. Whatever you've got. I'll take all of it."

"Ha, seriously though."

I stare at him, deadpan.

"Whoa," his face tightens. "I can't do that, kid. Bad for business."

"Moving all your product is bad for business?"

"Man, if I thought you were going to buy all my shit and do it responsibly then, yeah, that'd be solid. But anyone who says they're going to take all of my shit without even hearing what it is first, that's dangerous. I can't have you killing yourself on my shit, man."

"Man, I just want to get out of my head. I'll take what you'll sell me."

I leave with forty joints – thirty-eight after we smoke together, which is something I never understand but is part of the process of buying pot – twenty Percocet, and ten Viagra. He designs this combo pack so I can "keep mellow."

After two joints I buy a bouquet of flowers, then I drive by Tiffany's house, but she still isn't home so I take them to my mom.

In my room I divvy the drugs into separate baggies, something a respectable drug dealer should have done, and count the painkillers that remain from my leg surgery. They were so I could deal with walking on my shattered bone, but the pain made it easier than the pills. Every step rewarded me with a shuddering pain so intense I couldn't ignore it, but after months of walking on broken bones, I barely even limp.

I find Wayne's letter. Read it again. Take ten Percocet. Lie on the floor.

FIFTY-SEVEN

Tiffany's presents sit in an unmanageable pile on my dresser, wrapped in shimmering Christmas paper, bound in elegant bows. If money could guarantee affection, then she'd be in love.

In the few weeks since our discussion, I've grown increasingly anxious sitting alone in my room and getting high.

I want to call to make sure we're still on to celebrate together because the sun is setting, the day ending, but she said she'd call. I look through the texts that she's sent since winter break started: *I love you*, sent two days ago at two in the morning; *I miss you*, sent a week ago at six in the morning.

I shudder at the idea that she won't call even though this was her idea. I know she won't, no matter what I try to trick myself into thinking. So, I take a deep breath and call. A knot tightens in my stomach with each ring. She doesn't answer, and I'm verging on panic when she doesn't answer the second time I call, so I call again. She picks up on the fourth ring of the sixth call.

I wait for her to talk first, to hear her voice for the first time in weeks.

"Hi, Brody," she says.

"Hey," I stammer back.

"I was going to call you. How have you been?"

"Were you really going to call?"

"Of course."

"When?"

"I was just about to call you, Brody."

"I can't wait to bring you your presents."

"I was thinking that we should do that after Christmas."

"Then they wouldn't be Christmas presents," I say.

"I'm just so busy, Brody."

"Why do you keep saying my name?" I ask. Then, before she can answer, "This was your fucking idea. Do you want them or not?"

"Of course I do. I'm just busy."

"It'll take twenty minutes. I'll just drop them off and leave."

"No, Brody. We'll do it later."

I skip a beat. "Have you given any thought to our situation?"

"I don't want to talk about it right now." Her curtness tears through the euphoria of talking to her. I bite my lip to keep from talking, but can't stop myself.

"Can I just bring your presents over? Can I just see you?"

"I have to leave in about an hour. Let's do it after Christmas."

"If I don't come over now then we're done. This was your idea."

"Broderick, please don't." There is a strained and unfamiliar pleading in her voice.

"Why?"

"I don't want to see you. Do not come over. If that means we're done then that's your decision." I listen to the dial tone for almost a minute after she hangs up before I set the phone down.

I knew this would happen.

I blast the radio on the way to her house, so loud I can't think. A few blocks out, in the ascent of overtaking a junk heap of a car, I look over and do a double take before I let myself acknowledge the reason Tiffany didn't want me to come over.

I've seen him once, through a window, but I'll never forget his fucking face. I'm passing Wayne.

He looks ahead, completely unaware I'm studying him. A rag of curled, blonde hair nearly covers his tiny, beaded eyes. His Vienna sausage fingers wrap around the steering wheel and I imagine them wrapped around Tiffany's breasts, sinking into her body.

I slow to the speed limit and hide behind a car in the same lane as Wayne. I turn my music up louder, imagine the sound Wayne's fingers will make when I break them.

I hang back and watch as he pulls into her subdivision. When he parks I pull behind him so he can't back out.

I wait for him to get out of his car until I can't stand it anymore and then I pound on his window, screaming, "Get out, you fat mother fucker! Get out of your car so I can fucking kill you!"

I don't think about how nice Tiffany's neighborhood is, or my still-running car. I don't think about my future or Tiffany or justice or revenge or love or fidelity. I lose myself to muscle and sinew, to motion and rage.

When I punch his window, I slam every emotion I've ever felt into the glass, but it doesn't break.

His eyes grow wide with fear, like a deer in the path of a freight train. He fumbles to start his car, panics, and grinds over the curb to pull away from me, leaving me in the street, near feral, screaming nothing at the top of my lungs.

I throw myself into my car and tear backwards.

He isn't just her friend. He's everything I feared.

He made it easy for her to leave me, to replace me. In the last month of school I writhed in doubt and agony about her, hating myself for wanting her. She lied left and right about wanting to see me and still loving me.

When I saw him in her room, I should have lit the fucking dorm on fire.

He speeds away from her subdivision, rounding a corner too fast, and drives over a curb. He speeds to a red light. When he brakes, I accelerate and slam into his bumper, screaming at the top of my lungs as I shove him into oncoming traffic. He guns his engine.

I pursue.

Clenching the steering wheel, white-knuckled, I vault past the cars between us, closing the gap to follow his cowardice. My gas pedal flat against the floor, I clock eighty mph. I'm speeding in slow motion; every car I pass stands still.

When I close the gap, riding alongside his car, I feel like I just broke a fever; like I was sick and now I'm well. Like molting. I smile my ice pick grin and pull the steering wheel right to sideswipe him.

He swerves.

We lock eyes again and he speeds up. As he does, I slam hard on my brakes and U-turn into oncoming traffic. Wayne speeds off. I wish he were dead, but he isn't my priority.

A truck halts to a stop, running off the road to avoid collision. I bounce over the median and merge with traffic toward Tiffany's house. I don't slow down until I'm in her driveway, then I leave my car running again as I race to her door.

I exhale, teeth clenched, and try to steady myself. My nerves smolder, my skin a shell to raw emotion, tearing wildly and clawing at every crevice to escape and rampage through anything it touches.

I ring the doorbell.

Nothing happens.

I ring it again.

Flynn answers the door and stares at me with terrible awe. Tiffany's mom rips Flynn away from the door, chokes out the words, "She isn't here." She slams the door, bashing it against my fingers. My eyes stay trained on hers. I leave my fingers in the door as a wedge.

I ask stoically, "Is Tiffany available?"

Her mom sputters, half-screaming, "Get out of here! God, Brody, just leave or I'm going to call the police!"

Every muscle in my body tenses. Something terrible pulses through me and the boundaries between right and wrong dissolve completely.

Then, through the door, I hear Flynn crying.

My knuckles catch in the doorframe as I withdraw my hand. She slams the door and then the clicks of locks and deadbolts remind me that I'm standing on their porch, the police undoubtedly *en route*.

I try to leave but my synapses misfire, shooting waves of violent energy into rebellious muscles. I want to kick the door in. I want to punch a hole through the wall. I want to douse myself in gasoline and burn to nothing at her door.

But I'm not this guy.

I'm not a monster. I don't make children cry.

Tears roll off my checks. I realize my teeth are still clenched, my fists are still balled.

She doesn't love me.

After what feels like eternity I kick the railing off their porch and slink into my car. I round the corner and pull out of the subdivision. Red and blue lights blaze toward me. I exhale, steeling myself. I coast at the speed limit, then pull behind an SUV.

Three cop cars race past me. Anyone could have called, reported me or my car. I hold my breath and wait for them to U-turn into my lane, but they speed past.

I ease through traffic until I find an interstate, then get off onto Highway 65 and floor it.

FIFTY-EIGHT

It's nearly ten in the morning when I make it to the beach. I get an ocean-view room at the same hotel where Tiffany and I stayed when I proposed to her, leave the balcony door open, and let the sound of the ocean waves wash me to sleep.

I wake up to looming overcast. Gray clouds hang heavy over the water, and a rank ocean smell lingers in the air. I pull on my hoodie and head across the street to the liquor store where I grab a flask-sized bottle of Jim Beam.

"Hey, buddy. ID?" the cashier asks when I try to pay. I hand him another twenty with a blank stare and turn to leave. "Man, I can't sell you that if you aren't twenty-one."

"Do what you have to do," I say and leave.

From my balcony I watch the waves bounce off the shore. I drink until I have a solid buzz, then I get my phone from my car and turn it on.

It buzzes, beeps once, then twice, then six times in rapid succession. Four voicemails, all from Mom. Two texts, both Julia. One says, *Hey.* The other asks, *Have you ever been to Canada?*

I call her, but she doesn't answer. While the phone is ringing I get a text from Tiffany: *Are you okay?* I think about calling her, then take my phone apart and stash it in a drawer. I down the whiskey, then lie in bed listening to the waves.

The next day I realize I haven't eaten since I left, so I buy a bag of oranges and go back to the liquor store for another bottle of whiskey.

"Look, man," the same cashier says when I walk in, "I can't sell you anything. You need to go or I'm going to call the police."

I pull a handle of whiskey off the shelf and slap another fifty-dollar bill on the counter before I ask, "Would you rather I just stole it?"

Back in my room I refill the flask-sized bottle. I stuff it in my pocket and lean against the balcony railing as I take long, deliberate swigs from the jug. The beach is mostly deserted, probably because it's forty degrees and clouds hang ominous and purple like some kind of biblical warning.

As far as I can tell I'm the only person staying in the hotel.

I reassemble my phone and walk barefoot to the shore. The tide is coming in. I grind my toes into the sand. Waves pool gently around my feet, then retreat. I dig out a handful of sand, cupping it in my palm. The sand streams through my fingers, leaving only a thin layer of grit.

My phone buzzes with a new voicemail from Mom. I play the voicemails, listening to them in reverse order: "I'm going to call the police if you don't call me today." "Where are you?" "Where are you?" "Are you going to be home for Christmas?" "You need to call me."

The tide washes in farther with each wave. I dig my feet into the wet sand as I finish off my whiskey. A violent wave covers me in white foam, soaking my pants. I consider throwing the empty bottle into the ocean. I don't at first, thinking about recycling and pollution and then about the archaic message in a bottle and what a desperate gesture that is. But it starts to rain so I throw it in anyway, and I'm very satisfied with how seamlessly it disappears into the ocean.

FIFTY-NINE

I'm lying on my back in the sand when I get a text from my mom that reads *How could you do this to me?* and I realize it's Christmas day.

On the drive home I get a message from Tiffany that asks, *Are you okay? I just want to know.* I consider throwing my phone out the window, but instead send her one back that says, *Go fuck yourself.*
    Mom doesn't say a word to me when I get home. Doesn't chew me out. Doesn't wish me a merry Christmas. My father, though, takes the time to tell me, "You need to grow up, son."
    "Merry Christmas to you, too," I say, and retreat to my room where I grab what's left of my drugs. I pick piles of dirty clothes off the floor to stuff into a hamper to take with me, but realize I can just buy new clothes when I get to school so I leave them.
    I climb back into my car, which is filled with trash from my trip and box after box of Tiffany's presents. After driving thirteen hours home, being there just long enough to rub salt in my parents' disappointment, I don't know if I'll make it all the way back to school without crashing in some kind of narcoleptic coma, so I stop at a gas station and buy a sack full of energy drinks and beef jerky. Before I leave, I disappoint all the starving and less fortunate

children who did without this Christmas and toss a few thousand dollars worth of Tiffany's Christmas presents in the gas station dumpster.

Since school doesn't start until the middle of January the dorms are still closed when I get back to campus. I rent a hotel room that looks exactly the same as the one in Florida. I traded a beach-front balcony for a Jacuzzi, but otherwise functionally the same.

A maid wakes me up the next morning when she walks into my room. "I'm sorry," she says when she sees that I'm in. "I'll come back."

"No," I say. "Don't come back until I'm gone."

I hang the Do Not Disturb sign on the door and go back to sleep. I order a pizza when I get up and then brush my teeth and take a shower. When the pizza shows up I eat a few slices, then go swimming. The next day, I steam in the Jacuzzi and watch pay-per-view movies. A thick cloud of marijuana smog forms and, even though I run the bathroom fan, the smoke is so thick that I have to waft through it to see the TV.

I don't leave the room for a week. I've seen every pay-per-view movie on the hotel TV and stacked pizza boxes waist-high by the door.

A sort of desperation clings to my skin, the tepid clamp of dried sweat and anxiety.

I run out of pot at the beginning of the second week. After three full days without drugs, I realize I'm going to have to leave the hotel. I scroll through my cell's phonebook, calling anyone who could be on campus. Everyone I call is out of town, so I keep the conversations short and pretend that I just called to say hey.

Davis is one of the last names on my list. I don't know him that well, but at this point it's worth a shot.

"My dealer is on vacation," he says, "but come on over and let's find something to get into."

I stop at a department store before I go and buy a new outfit. I change in my car and leave the dirty clothes that I've been wearing for the last few weeks on the floor.

Davis greets me with a near-freezing can of beer. His face is powerful, believable, but it has a worn-out sheen that undermines him.

"I'm glad you called, man. I've been feeling awfully clandestine."

I nod and crack the beer. He produces two joints.

"Two left," he says, handing me my own. This seems very gracious considering the way people share joints, suckling a stranger's spit for a chance to feel a little more detached than usual.

"I'll pay you for this," I say as I help myself to another beer.

"Not even, man. Help yourself."

"Well," I say, "a friend of mine gave me some Viagra. I'm not going to do anything with them. You want them?" I hand him the bag. Fair enough trade, I imagine.

"Sure," he says, inspecting the bag. "They work?"

"Haven't tried."

"Every man must know his limitations," he says and pops two of them.

"Shit, dude."

"Relax. They don't make you hard unless you would be anyway." He hands me the bag. "I'm going to call some friends over. Take some. Let's see what happens."

I swallow a knot in my throat and choke out, "I'm good."

"Come on, Brody."

I roll the dice and take two of them. He slides his cell phone open and sends a text, which is answered by a series of beeps. I down another beer and watch the shitty movie he's got playing on TV while he texts.

Two beers later the doorbell rings, and Davis answers to two girls who walk in and introduce themselves.

"Stacy" is tall and thin and plain.

"Jane" is less plain, even a little ugly in a way that works for her, with ghost-white skin and black hair.

Davis hands them the bag. They swallow the pills without even asking what they are. "So," Jane says, her voice deep and throaty, "you're just sitting around trying to pop boners?"

I sigh and get another beer.

"Be a gentleman and get me one too," Jane says. When I hand it to her she leans in close and sniffs me, then takes a drink and says, "You smell like a department store."

"Pheromones," I say.

We drink for a while. Stacy and Davis banter. Every giggle and laugh and inside joke annoys me. Stacy laughs at her own jokes, which makes my skin crawl. I grab another beer. When I find my way back to the living room, Davis has restarted the movie that's been on since I got here.

"How can you watch this over and over?" I ask.

"Stacy hasn't seen it yet." He motions to her like an excuse.

"Well, I have," I say. "I'm going back to the hotel. I can't watch this again."

Jane stops me. "You shouldn't drive."

"I'm fine," I say.

"No, she's right, Brody," Davis says.

"How many has he even had?" Stacy says to Davis.

He shrugs.

"We'll take your car," Jane says.

I'm probably fine, but after my accident drunk

driving just doesn't seem worth it so I cave and hand Jane the keys.

Davis nods at me, a half-smile on his face reading like a *You're welcome*.

Jane invites herself up. She has a bottle of vodka in her purse, so I let her in.

In the soft light of the hotel room, Jane strips naked and drops her underwear in a crumpled pile by the hot tub. She pulls her hair into a bun and climbs in with a simple kind of slyness, a look on her face that says C*ome and get me*.

I get a jolt of dread about the possibility that I'll fuck her. I watch her for a second as I dry-swallow a Percocet and then strip and climb into the hot tub, positioning myself so she can't see my scars. We sit on opposite sides of the tub in the boiling water. There is a thick and tangible tension that rises with the steam. She slides closer to me. Suddenly, she grabs my wrist and pulls my arm close to her for inspection. "What happened to your arm?"

"I was attacked by a bear on a Boy Scout trip."

She looks at my leg. "Liar. These look self-inflicted."

"Nope." I pull my arm away. "Bear attack."

I climb out of the tub and dig through my bag for the painkillers. I pop four of them, crunch them and let the bitter chalky taste cover my tongue, then I fall into the bed, soaking the sheets, and hold the bag of pills out to Jane as a peace offering.

She turns them down, then lies next to me and tries to suck me off, but nothing happens. "Are you okay?" she asks. "Are you not attracted to me?"

I'm not sure if she's still talking when I fall asleep.

SIXTY

When the dorms open, I buy some new clothes and check out of the hotel. The room feels colder than usual, and Ken is gone, so I take Ken's blanket and use both of them until he gets back.

On the first day of class I wake up early and take a shower and go to the cafeteria to eat breakfast. I go to class early and hang out in the quad on my breaks. For the first week, I eat every meal in the cafeteria with Ken or Cynthia, and I pass Tiff's dorm on the way to the gym.

Without realizing it, I fall back into the same routine that I had with Tiffany.

I start to notice the empty seat between me and Cynthia at dinner. I think about the night I saw Wayne every time I pass her window.

After a week, I stop leaving my room except to go to class.

I don't know what makes it so easy for other people to cope with shit like this, eat a pint of ice cream or whatever people do and move on.

I wonder if our relationship had ever been important to her or if I destroyed it.

With Valerie, I watched that relationship die. I killed it. I fought with her every day about whatever bullshit I pretended justified me being mad. When I broke up with her I thought she'd eventually realize how bad I made her feel, but the next day she was dead.

And I'll never know if it was because of me or in spite of me.

But Tiffany – I don't understand what happened. I knew she was a cheater when I started dating her, and I don't know why but I thought that I'd be different.

Part of me wishes Tiffany were dead. If she had killed herself I'd be rejected, not replaced. And by that fat piece of shit, Wayne.

I keep imagining his fat, greasy hands all over Tiffany.

By the third week of school I stop going to class at all.

SIXTY-ONE

Julia leans forward on her bench in front of our dorm wearing a fur-lined parka and sandals, breathing smoke out into air cold enough I can see her breath from here. Her footprints lead from a wad of diesel-black snow piled against the curb to the bench.

Something about the scene bothers me, like it always does. I watch her as I microwave a half-drunk cup of day-old coffee. She seems as out of place on that bench, waiting for whomever or whatever, as she does in class or any other time that I've ever seen her.

I text her: *Want to hang out?*

She flips open her phone, then folds it back into her pocket without responding. I open the window to yell down to her, but cold air rushes in and I change my mind.

I dump the coffee in the sink and take a shower.

Afterward, I walk back into the room with only a towel draped around my waist. Ken and Julia sit on opposite beds.

"Ken let me in," Julia says. "Why didn't you tell me he was your roommate when we talked about Voodoo Lounge?"

I shrug. Fucking Ken.

I dress quickly, still damp, beads of water saturating my clothes.

"Well." Ken stands up and walks to the door. "I

just stopped up here for my wallet." He points at me, raising his eyebrows. "Dinner?"

I shake my head.

"Want me to bring you something back from the cafeteria?"

I shake my head again.

He pats the door and disappears.

Fucking Ken.

Julia lies back across my bed, her slender frame engulfed by the monstrous parka. "You seem weirder than usual," she says with a coy smile. I lean against the wall and study her delicate features, thin lips, and sad eyes.

"Yeah," I croak.

"Are you okay?" she asks.

I stare at her until I realize she wants an answer.

"I'm going to get drunk. You want to?" I blurt, desperate to kill any chance of conversation.

"Sure," she says. As she sits up, her hair falls to frame her face.

I clasp my hands together and nod, relieved, then grab Ken's gin from under the sink. Ken is the only person I've ever met who likes gin, mostly because it's shit. But that's what he has, so I grab two bottles of his Mountain Dew from the mini fridge, empty one completely before I look back to her and ask, "Chaser?" She shakes her head and purses her lips. I fill both bottles with equal parts gin and Mountain Dew, hand one off, and we each suck back the first bitter gulp.

With the drink in my hand, I can relax. We sit in comfortable silence.

"Let's go for a walk," she says.

Outside, a soft sprinkle of flurries falls, obscuring her old footprints. We make fresh tracks as we walk through campus. In an alley between the music and art buildings I stop to take a swig of gin, barely able to pull the bottle from my lips before Julia grabs the lapel of my peacoat and kisses me softly. I drop the bottle and grab her waist, pulling her into me as we kiss.

"I have something I need to tell you before we go any further," I say, standing shirtless in a new, exactly-the-same hotel room.

"Um," she hesitates, "what?" She brings her arms up to cover her breasts as she says this, sits back against the headboard in her underwear.

"I, um. Fuck." I unbutton my pants. "I'll just show you."

As I slide my pants off, revealing the bands of purple scarring, her eyes grow wide. I get a vague feeling of déjà vu as she leans over, rubs my leathery skin and says "Oh my fucking God" real low, talking to herself.

"What are these long ones from?" she asks, running her thumb down the plastic skin of my surgery scars. "You didn't do these to yourself too. You couldn't have."

"Car wreck," I say.

"What happened?"

"Drunk driver."

"Is that why you limp?" she asks.

I nod.

"Wow."

I brush a strand of hair from Julia's face and take her to bed.

It's strange: the things people will tell you once you've had sex. Like, it lifts a veil under which they carry their darkest moments. Maybe people just want to connect. Maybe they don't want to feel alone. Maybe they just want someone to understand.

Whatever the reason, Julia tells me things I've

never heard before: how she was basically a sex slave for this couple in Arizona and how she did ecstasy every day for a year straight.

Lying naked in the hotel bed, she tells me about how her dad hasn't been around in forever, but that he sends her flowers out of the blue. She tells me stories about her old friends, how one of them went to prison and left her Chihuahua with her boyfriend and the boyfriend threw it against the wall over and over again until he killed it. Her skin glows as she recounts memories, each more terrible than the last, and there is something beautiful about it.

"What do you like about me?" I ask her.

"Who says I like you?" She grins.

I run my fingers along her neck and say, "Seriously."

"There's a lot to like about you," she says, "like how you're basically the only guy I know who'd take a girl to a hotel room to fuck her instead of just expecting it to happen at the dorms."

"I was really asking," I say.

"You know what attracted me to you the minute I saw you? Your eyes. And I don't mean it like everyone else says it." She turns her body toward me. Her hand on my cheek. "I think sadness is beautiful, and there's so much of it in your eyes."

We talk for hours, and I start to wonder if that's the point of sex: if we get so close so we can really connect to each other. I talk until she stops responding, her breath suddenly heavy. When I realize she's asleep, I roll over. Her arm hangs limply over my neck, revealing four faded scars across her wrist.

SIXTY-TWO

I take Julia out for breakfast the next morning, thinking we'd see each other later, but then we spend all morning together in my room listening to music that I hate.

We lie together on my twin bed, her small, weightless body curled around me.

Around noon I suggest we get some food and take her out for Mexican.

I'm mid-bite into a burrito at a Mexican restaurant when this Bohemian-looking girl drops by the table.

"Julia," she says, "how have you been?" Then the girl drops her sunglasses to her nose to eyeball me.

Julia smiles, kind of. "Yeates," she says. "Good. Really good." She nods to punctuate her goodness. I tear another chunk out of the burrito.

"Well, aren't you going to introduce me to your friend?" Yeates asks, shifting her weight to look at me, hand on her hip, striking a pose in her knee-length hemp coat-sweater. I choke down the food in my mouth without chewing.

"Brody," I say.

"You were in that play, weren't you?" she asks excitedly.

I nod.

"Where are my manners?" she asks herself.

"Everyone calls me Yeates." She shifts her attention to Julia and says, "I'm having a little get-together at my place. You two should come."

"Maybe," Julia returns. "Who's going to be there?"

Yeates rests her hand on Julia's shoulder. "It's just a little thing." She looks at me and says, "I have to run though." Back to Julia she adds "Call me" as she backs out through the door.

"She's off," I say, taking another bite.

"She did seem off," Julia says, pushing her food away.

"Do you want to go?"

"No," she says.

"I'll go if you want to go."

"I don't."

"Well, if you change your mind."

"Fine," she says. "Let's go."

Julia raps on the door and Yeates invites us into her apartment on the second floor of a coin laundromat between a pawn shop and a liquor store. Julia and Yeates air-kiss, which makes me want to throw up, so I slide behind them and stand in the living room. I've heard people tell each other to never buy furniture in a college town because someone is always throwing it out.

This whole apartment was thrown out.

A stick of a girl offers her hand in an imitation of a shake. "Hi. I'm Grace."

I half hold it, half shake it, as I introduce myself. Yeates pours drinks and we all sit in the living room. Julia sits across from me. I look at her and nod to the spot next to me on the couch, but she shakes her head.

I look from Yeates to Grace to Julia and ask, "Are we early?"

Yeates shakes her head and pulls a vinyl record out of its sleeve on her bookshelf. "There's someone else coming still. It's a surprise," she says and drops the needle to play "One Headlight" by The Wallflowers.

Grace grazes my calf with her foot and I ignore it. Then she stands up to adjust the needle on the record player, restarting the song. Upon return she brushes my knee, then sits in the middle of the futon right next to me.

"So." I look at Yeates. "What do you study?"

Before Yeates can answer, Grace blurts, "Let's get some cocaine!"

A few minutes later, Grace stands behind me, drunk, while I withdraw three hundred dollars from an ATM.

"Do you think I'm pretty?" she asks.

I ignore her and fold the cash into my pocket. "Where now?" I ask.

She gives me directions to a quiet neighborhood where I park under a street light. "B.R.B.," she says as I hand her the money. Then she walks behind a house and disappears. I turn on the radio and wait.

I almost don't hear my phone vibrating when Julia texts me.

Don't say anything. Then *Please* in a separate message. I'm staring at the messages when Grace knocks on the window. I open the door and she plops into the seat. She's obviously high and her hair is out of place like she's been having sex.

"Go okay?" I ask.

She nods and hands me a tiny, white rock wrapped in cellophane.

In the apartment, Julia sits in the lap of a tall, flat-faced, frat-looking guy. She passes me a terrified, almost pleading glance. "Broderick," she says, "this is

Brian." Her voice raises an octave as she adds, "My boyfriend."

I have to question if this was the point of my wasted evening. Maybe Yeates saw me with Julia and through some thought process I don't quite understand meant to drop us both in a tank with Brian and watch drama unfold in her own little black-box play.

Brian reaches for my hand. "Julia has told me a lot about you."

Don't say anything.

Like I wouldn't know better.

I smile and shake his hand as my brittle heart crumbles into dust and blows away, nothing but black powder. I'm the intruder here. I'm Wayne.

I look at Julia and ask, "So are we going to do some coke?"

"How much did you get?" Julia asks.

I produce the rock. Brian nods his approval. "Nice. That's like four grams." He cuts it up with his credit card, shaving off six lines of powder. Julia rolls a dollar bill into a straw and snorts a line, then immediately does another.

"Whoa there," Brian chuckles.

He does a line. Then Yeates. Then Grace.

I kneel down by the coffee table. When I snort my first line I cough, spraying cocaine mist across the table. Maybe half the line makes it into my nose, but it's enough.

An explosion sets off.

A gentle angelic strumming.

A wild burst of energy.

Julia, her soft lips curled into a pucker, asks, "What do you think?"

"My eyes feel like they're wired into a car battery."

As soon as the powder hits my nose I feel alive in a way I can't explain. I feel – I know – I could do anything. Brian cuts out more lines. I watch him, cutting my coke up, and I guess it's a kind of peace offering for fucking his girlfriend. Brian, this guy I've never met before and suddenly I'm fucking his life up.

"I need to go outside," I say, springing off the couch.

On the porch I bounce on the balls of my feet, let myself cave to the sudden urge to call Tiffany. As the phone rings, I gather a snowball and throw it across the laundromat parking lot at a vagrant cat. The endless ringing has become so familiar; for months it was the closest I'd come to connecting to her.

Her machine picks up and I listen to the message, intending to apologize to her, but then someone picks up and Tiffany tiredly rasps "Hello?" over the answering machine.

I didn't expect her to answer; I don't have anything to say.

Julia opens the door and steps out onto the porch.

I panic and hang up.

"Who was that?" Her dragon's breath hangs hot in the cold air.

"You know," I lean away from her, "this." I motion toward the door. "That. You might have mentioned it before this."

"I know." She shrugs and bites her lip. "By the way, you missed a step. After you take the bump, you rub what's left on your gums." She shows me the patina of cocaine on her fingers, then rubs her middle finger in my mouth and then her index finger in her own.

My mouth goes numb. Tastes like the static on TV. I think about kissing her, then remember seeing Wayne in Tiffany's window. I bum a cigarette and we stand on the snowy porch smoking. Her eyes are so wide. I touch her hand and can feel it in my veins.

Brian opens the door, his face flushed, and says,

"Let's get out of here. I've still got people to see tonight."

"Yeah," she nods at him. "Bye, Brody."

They start down the stairs and I walk inside without responding. Yeates and Grace are dancing to a new song, something I don't know with a heavy beat that makes me feel like dancing, too. Instead I cut out a line twice the size of Brian's and snort it. Then another one. Then another one.

The record skips.

Yeates, still dancing, says, "Thanks for buying us coke." She's jumping around her room as she asks, "Are you and Julia an item or just friends? I mean, I thought you were an item when I saw you out with her and thought she was being shady so I invited Brian to come surprise her. So, like, you aren't an item obviously, but she kept staring at the door when you were outside and she normally isn't like that. Plus she kept talking about you when you were gone."

When I don't respond, Yeates, who meant to drop me and Brian in the same tank like betta fish, asks, "You want another drink?"

"Yeah," I say.

She dances over to the kitchen and Grace sits on the floor, cutting lines. I don't know either of these girls, but they treat me like I'm a childhood friend. Grace, sitting in front of ten rows of white friendship, looks up at me with light-bulb eyes and asks, "Want to hit it first?"

I do.
I hit it first.
Then she does.
Then Yeates hands me a drink and takes a hit.

The drink is as strong as rubbing alcohol, and I love it.

Yeates hits another greedy line and changes the record. Then Grace sits next to me on the couch, touching my thigh. Her shirt is cut so low that I barely notice when she asks, "So where are you from?"

"Louisville."

"I'm from Chicago," she starts. "It's nothing like here. I don't even know why I'm at this school most of the time. Kentucky is such a rat's nest. There's nothing to do here at all." She only asked me where I'm from so she could trash Kentucky.

"Have you ever done any modeling?" I ask her drunkenly. "You could be a model." Then I do another line.

She says, without skipping a beat, "I've done some modeling." She does a line.

"Really? How much weight have you gained since?" Her ribs show through her skintight shirt and protrude like ornaments beneath her clavicle. The glitter falls out of her eyes.

I do another line.

Yeates's boyfriend calls at around three a.m., so she leaves Grace and I to what's left of the coke. The record plays out and static serenades us while we sit awkwardly on the couch. I get up to leave and she walks me to the door, then grabs my wrist before she pulls off her shirt, tosses it to the floor, and asks, "Do you really think I'm fat?"

I throw my hands up in mock defeat. "No."

She pops off her bra and closes the door. We have sex like thunder and she runs her hands over my face saying, "You're so beautiful." When I'm about to come, she whispers "I love you" in my ear and I lose it.

SIXTY-THREE

I wake up coughing so intensely that I have to stand up to keep from choking. I cover my mouth, and when I've caught my breath I see my hand is covered in blood.

I blow my nose. Long strings of bloody mucus trail to the tissue. Blood leaks from my nose like a faucet.

Grace stirs restlessly when I shake her. "What the fuck is this?" I half shout. "Were we snorting fucking glass?"

She looks at me, nonplussed, through her bloodshot eyes. "It was harsh, I guess," she says and rolls over.

There's a strange haze between us, like I shouldn't be there and we both know it. I slide into my jeans and walk onto the balcony to call Julia. I remember that Tiffany answered last night, and I almost call her. I linger on her number until I realize what I'd say. "Hey, I spent all night doing coke and fucked a total stranger. How have you been?"

I call Julia instead.

"God damn. I feel like my eyes are about to fall out of my head. I don't think I can drive. Will you come get me?" I ask. Someone drags a basket of laundry through the parking lot. I should have put a shirt on.

"I know it seems tough, but you'll feel better when you get in the car. Just man up."

She hangs up.

I get dressed. Find my keys and wallet. The rock is still on their coffee table, half of it powdered and smeared in thick swipes. I take the solid part and lock the door on my way out.

SIXTY-FOUR

Ken is brushing his teeth when I get up.

Since I lost track of time, since I stopped going to class, I use Ken's habits as my sun dial. If Ken gets dressed for class it means that it's almost bedtime. When Ken brushes his teeth, then I start thinking about getting out for the night. If I've eaten all of Ken's food out of the fridge, then it's time to run to Arby's and buy fifteen beef and cheddar sandwiches.

My eyes adjust and I sit up.

"I was starting to wonder if you were dead," Ken says.

I run my finger around my mouth and inspect it for blood. "Have you ever done coke?"

He stares back at me through the mirror and laughs.

"You'd like it."

"You're not kidding? Fuck that," he says. "Brody, I barely even smoke pot."

"You smoke it enough."

"I only smoke pot with you." He checks his hair and puts on his shoes. "By the way, do you have any? Cynthia wants some."

"It feels like I haven't seen her in weeks," I say as I dig a bag of weed out of my drawer.

"You have to stay connected, man." He turns away from the mirror. "How do I look?"

"Dynamite." I toss him the bag.

"I'll wait if you want to come out with us. My friend's band is playing at The Voodoo Lounge."

"I have things to which I must attend, Ken. Next time."

"Well. We should hang out soon." He grabs his keys and wallet. "I feel like I never see you anymore."

I nod. He leaves.

I spend most of the night watching porn. At three in the morning I figure Ken isn't coming back and I'll have the room to myself, so I pull my X-Acto knives out of the drawer and sit on my bed to cut myself. I pick a thin carving blade and drag it across my thigh. The cut is light. It barely bleeds, so I do it again.

I cut myself seven times, but they're only skin deep and don't hurt enough to make me feel anything. I pull my jeans back on and watch as tiny spots bleed through the fabric. I lie back, deflated, and sigh.

I grab my coat and walk to the back entrance of Tiffany's dorm. There's no reason she'd want to talk to me again after the scene I made at her house, much less be with me. But, in everything I do, I have a whispering feeling under my skin that she should be there or that I should be at her door waiting until she changes her mind.

I light a cigarette and wait by the door until some guy walks up and slides his keycard to open the door. I hold it open and put my cigarette out, smiling as natural as if I live here. I walk up to Tiff's room and knock. When she doesn't answer I call her room phone and listen through the door until her answering machine picks up. I wait for any sign she's there, but all I hear is the stupid fucking machine. I call her cell. I listen for a ring through the door, but there isn't one, so I leave.

SIXTY-FIVE

After some inane back and forth, Grace agrees to middle-man for me buying coke. Her dealer, she says, won't deal with new people.

She meets me at my dorm and I hand her the money.

"How can you drop so much on coke?" she asks.

"How much does that get me?"

"A shit load," she says. "I don't know exactly."

"Well, some of it's yours. That's the deal."

"Brody, I don't know if he'll even have this much."

There's a tax when you do anything black market. I know that from James. There's always someone on the logistics chain taking his own cut. The trick, I think, is that I don't care. She'll take what she wants, but she'd take it anyway, and it's not like they sell coke at convenience stores.

"I'll call you when I've got it," she says.

A few days later she calls. I meet Grace in the parking lot. Her hair and makeup are immaculate, a far cry from the Bohemian act she put on the last time I saw her. I'm not prepared for the weather to still be so cold, so I turn around to go back to my room and get my coat. While I'm waiting for the elevator, Julia steps out of it. Her face lights up when she sees me.

"Let's go get dinner," she says, touching my arm. I

haven't talked to her since she told me to man up.

"Yes," I say emphatically as I step into the elevator. If she steps outside she'll see Grace waiting in her car, and I don't want to deal with that so I say, "I'm going to grab my wallet. Wait for me here. I'll be right down."

I get my jacket, leave my cell phone in my room in case Julia calls, and take the steps to the side door so I'll miss her on my way out.

Grace drives about a half hour outside of the city into some desolate woods, grinding over off-roads to park in an alcove of trees. We sit in silence while she packs a pipe.

"Here." She hands me a substantial rock of cocaine. "That should last you a while."

There's not much room to argue. She takes a deep puff off the pipe and passes it to me. A blood moon hangs low in the sky, stark against a roll of thin clouds.

"Everyone acts like we're so different," she starts out of nowhere, "but we're not. I mean, you look around and the people you see, they've all been through shit. Everyone acts like they've had it worse, like their shit is so bad. But you, you act like no one has ever gone through any bad shit but you."

She just keeps going. It's like, because she's hot, no one has ever taken the time to stop her mid-sentence and say, "I'm not that interested in what you have to say. Truncate it and get back to me." But I don't stop her either.

"And people tell me to stay away from you," she says before looking to me for a reaction, some kind of dramatic explosion in self-defense. "But I think there's something... special about you." She emphasizes *special*, pronouncing each word with crystal clarity like she's in an MTV reality show confessional booth.

"Pass me the pipe," I say.
She does.

SIXTY-SIX

I'm lying in bed twirling a thin X-Acto knife and thinking about arterial veins when someone bangs on my door. I drop the knife in a drawer and lumber across the room.

"What the fuck is your problem?" Julia hisses as I open the door.

I lean against the doorframe and yawn.

"I was down there for forty-five minutes before I realized you weren't coming back, you bastard."

"Sorry."

"Fuck your 'sorry,' you arrogant bastard. I thought you were better than that shit." She furrows her brow and I realize this is the first time I've seen her angry. I grab her waist and kiss her. She pushes me off, but I pull her into my room, letting the door slam as I kiss her more furiously. She can't pull my clothes off fast enough as we fall into my bed.

Afterward, we're lying in my twin bed, our bodies pressed together, and Julia whispers, "Let's get some coke."

"How do you think your boyfriend would feel about that?"

She sits up, covering her breasts with my sheet. "Don't do that to me."

"You should've told me."

"Fine. I'm sorry. We're even. Can we please get

some coke?"

"I don't feel like it," I lie.

"Please?" she whines. "I've wanted it since last week." Four or five grams of cocaine is hidden in my sock drawer, but I let her bargain. "I'll fuck you."

"You just fucked me!" I produce the rock and toss it in her lap. Her face lights up like a Disney princess's.

I cut a few lines and we snort them off the dresser.

While I'm cutting another line, Julia gets a text inviting her to a party and I suddenly realize I want to be outside. I want to be at a party.

On the way out of the room I catch my reflection in the mirror and can't help but notice how anemic I look.

Julia cranes her neck and says, "That one," pointing at a strip of cheap townhouses.

"Which one?" I ask. "You're pointing at nothing."

"The only one with a red light."

Pounding on the apartment door, the music is so loud I can barely hear Julia tell me to stop. No one answers anyway. I tuck my thumbs in my pockets and rock back and forth. Julia texts the host and the door opens almost instantly. This lizard-eyed hipster steps out and Julia hugs him and he hugs her back and I can't help but think that she's fucked him.

She doesn't introduce me.

There are maybe ten people in the apartment huddling around a plastic coffee table, snorting coke and listening to music.

These people are familiar, but I've never met them and I don't want to. In this room I feel as isolated as I ever have.

Every noise in the apartment is drowned out by the music. I have no idea why they're even staring at the TV because I know they can't hear it. Julia says something to me and I can't hear her so I just nod and she smiles and walks into another room.

Each line of coke, each bump, has a lifespan of about fifteen minutes and mine needs a refresher so I join the huddled crowd and kneel down to take a bump. This guy sitting across from me on the couch, he's wearing these cheap-looking aviator sunglasses and he smiles at me as I'm coming up from my line, breathing life in, and says to me, "Ah, synchronicity. Our destinies are intertwined," like it's supposed to make any sense, only it does.

It really fucking does.

"Nice glasses," I say.

"You like 'em? Man, they're yours," he says, cool and slow. He slides the aviators off his face, revealing bloodshot eyes so dilated I can't tell what color they are. He holds them out to me like they were always mine and I complete the sacred ritual, the bequeathing of power, by putting them on.

"That's a good look on you," this girl next to him says, leaning into him, her pupils just as dilated.

"Thanks," I say, genuinely indebted. "Really."

"Pass it forward, dude," he says. "Just love."

Davis texts me: *My house*. I stand up, leaving my nameless friends to find Julia.

It's a two-bedroom apartment. I peek outside to see if she's smoking, then through the first open bedroom door, into the bathroom, and when I can't find her I try to open the closed bedroom door. It's locked. I knock on it and she opens it immediately.

"Let's get out of here," I say.

"Yeah," she says, nodding.

The guy, now wearing fake vampire teeth, hands her a baggy full of pills.

"You want me to pay for those?" I ask.

She shakes her head and pulls me toward the

door as the novelty vampire closes his door.

Davis hugs Julia, then shakes my hand and asks, "How you doing?"

"Coming down, man."

"Um, is that good? Bad?" he asks, looking to the side to see my eyes behind my sunglasses. "You know it's like one in the morning, right?" He hands me a beer.

I show him the coke.

"Ohh," he says.

"Want to?"

We walk through his guests, stopping on the way to shake hands with some people I know, smile at some people I don't know. Davis opens the bathroom door; a blonde girl is giving someone head while he sits on the toilet. We bypass and walk into his room.

I cut some really fat lines. We snort them and I cut some more. I can almost feel my pupils dilate behind my glasses, remembering that our destinies, they are intertwined.

Julia does another line and says, "I'm going to mingle." She kisses my cheek and disappears. I cut out two more lines.

"Are you banging Julia?" Davis asks. Snorts.

"Why?" Another line.

"Never mind."

I pocket the coke and we rejoin the party.

Julia's talking to a skeletal theatre girl. I smile at her. She ignores me. I help myself to another beer. One of the more popular theatre kids walks up to me and asks, "Where's the cocaine?"

"Davis has it." He turns and disappears without responding.

I look around the apartment at these people who I half-know from class or plays or maybe have just stood next to in an elevator, transformed into cocaine vampires, drunk with possibility and disaffection, and think to myself that this world must exist solely in the night.

SIXTY-SEVEN

I have a midterm test in one of my classes, so I wake up to leave before the hotel's checkout. Julia is asleep in my shirt, wrapped in sheets and curled into a ball. I splash cold water on my face and then force her small t-shirt on.

I leave a note.

```
BABE,
   CLASS.
-BRODY
```

I wear my new sunglasses into class and take a seat by the door. The air is tepid and stale, but I swallow it anyway. My mouth feels like a trash can filled with sand.

The slob in front of me passes the test and Scantron form over his shoulder. I haven't seen any of this information and I don't know any of the terminology – this is only the third time I've come to this class all semester – so I start bubbling circles at random on the answer sheet.

I'm halfway through the test when a spot of blood drips from my nose onto the form, landing with a delicate plop. I wipe the blood with my finger, smearing it across the bubbles. Another drop splats on the sheet. I wipe my hand under my nose and when I pull it back my hand is covered with blood.

I pinch my nose to stop the flow as I walk through the desks to hand my test to the professor. Blood rolls down my hand and drips from my forearm and lands on the tile with the same incessant splat.

"I've gotta go," I say as I hand him the form. He looks at me in my aviators and unwashed hair, blood dripping all over Julia's skin-tight t-shirt. He doesn't say anything, so I turn around and just leave.

SIXTY-EIGHT

"Let's go to the cafeteria," Ken says on a rare morning that our paths cross.

"Too many people," I say, exaggerating my drawl as I pull my blanket over my face.

"What about Burger King, then?"

"No thanks," I say as I sit up.

"You know Robert Downey Jr.?" Ken asks, sitting cross-legged on his bed.

"The actor?"

"He used to be really fucked up on drugs. One night, he's got, like, ten felonies worth of coke in the trunk of his car and he stops for Burger King.

"Anyway, he says it saved his life. The burger was so bad that it freaked him out, like it was a bad omen or something. So he threw all his drugs in a river and decided then and there to get clean."

He stands up and gets his keys. "You sure you don't want some?"

I shake my head and roll away again, then listen as Ken opens and closes the door.

Around two p.m. sun slithers in through the window, crawling over my face and into my eyes. The heater is out, the constant hum replaced by a static quiet. I brush my teeth, watching my lips in the mirror as they contort around the brush, and notice that Ken has left a paper Burger King sack on my desk with a sticky note that reads: *I hope this is the worst burger you ever eat.*

Fucking Ken.

I peel the wrapper off and take a bite, letting the soggy burger mingle with the taste of mint toothpaste. I swallow it, then drop the burger back in the sack.

Suddenly, for absolutely no reason, I break down in tears. I crush the burger inside the sack, feeling it reduce to paste. I have to get the fuck out of this room. I have to breathe in air that no one has lived in.

Julia, in the courtyard sitting on that fucking bench, stops sipping her iced coffee when she sees me.

"What's wrong with you?" she asks.

"I need to get out of here. Want to go to Louisville with me?"

"Sure," she says. She pulls the lid from her drink and plucks an ice cube to pop into her mouth.

"Get in the car."

"I need to pack a bag at least," she says.

"I'll buy you new clothes," I say. "I'm leaving now."

"Okay, then," she says and follows me to the car, still suckling at her coffee.

SIXTY-NINE

"Who's your friend?" Mom asks me in the morning.

"She's my girlfriend," I say. It's not true, but it's less complicated. Sometimes lying is just easier.

Julia walks into the kitchen, brushing off sleep. I smile at her and offer her some orange juice.

"Julia," she says, holding her hand out to Mom.

"Nice to meet you."

Julia turns to me. "Where can I take a shower, honey bunny?"

I point her down the hall.

When she hears the shower running, Mom asks, "What happened to Tiffany?"

"Well, boyfriend," Julia says once we're in the car, "what are we doing today?"

"You aren't going to let that slide, are you?"

"Don't you want to be my boyfriend?"

"Let's go to the mall. I want to buy you something for you to wear to dinner later."

"Can't argue with that," she says.

The day before we drove well into the night, smoking pot and listening to the radio. Today, in the mall, I follow her around with my credit card. We hop from store to store as she picks clothes out and models them for me.

"Do you like this?" she asks, holding up underwear in a lingerie store.

"I won't know until I see it on you."

We shop until she gets hungry. When we leave, as I'm putting all of her shit in the trunk, she hugs me and says, "Thank you," and it's worth it.

We pass Valerie's cemetery on the way to lunch. I consider showing Julia the grave, but I haven't mentioned Valerie, even in passing. Instead I take her to the waterfront and we get lunch.

"You know what'd be funny?" she says, leaning over the table.

"What?"

"You still have Tiffany's ring, right?"

I nod.

"When we go out to dinner, we should go to the nicest place in town and you should ask me to marry you. Make a big scene." I don't respond and she leans farther. "Not for real, obviously. Like a scene. Acting."

I get a hotel room downtown and watch Julia slip into this red dress I bought her. Black pumps. Dangling earrings.

What Julia doesn't think about, smearing her new makeup all over her face, is that I didn't earn a cent of what I have. Normally someone trades away hours of his life to buy these things, impress his friends, feel important.

What Julia doesn't think about, smacking her lips together with her new lipstick, is that each dollar I spend was consolation for my blood and bone.

"Ready," she says, glossy from head to toe like a magazine ad.

I take her to a fancy sushi place and we sit at the bar while we wait for our table. I slip the bartender a fifty-dollar bill so he'll serve us, and I have a pretty thick buzz by the time we're seated.

"What's going on with you?" Julia asks. "Leaving school in a hurry. Buying out the mall for me."

"I don't know. It's like, have you ever watched a flock of birds swarm a pile of garbage?"

She shakes her head no. The waiter comes by again and we order.

"Well, that's what my life is like. A thousand birds descending into a dumpster."

She props her arm on the table and leans her head against it. "Are you the birds or the garbage?" she asks.

"Just the experience. My life is like watching birds swarm garbage."

"Wow," she says, sipping her drink. "I have no idea what that means."

I drop the subject.

The sun set while we were eating, so I drop one arm of my sunglasses behind the collar of my shirt as we leave and wear them like an ornament. We try getting into a bar, but they won't serve me so we walk farther down the street; Bardstown Road is restaurant after boutique after bar and repeat. We walk down the road until we find an Irish bar where the bartender looks distracted. We grab stools and hail her attention. She's frazzled and barely looks in our direction as Julia and I order more cocktails.

While we're waiting, Julia gets a call. She looks at me a little worried, then says, "I have to take this."

"Brian?"

She gets up without answering me. The bartender drops our drinks off. I down mine and lean back, looking to see where she went. Across the room, through a mass of bar skanks, I notice this guy in thick sunglasses looking my way. I can't place him but he's déjà vu familiar.

He notices me looking at him and cocks his head to the side. I look away, but he walks over and pulls

Julia's stool out to sit next to me. "What's it been," he says, "about a year and a half?" He drops his glasses, revealing small, bloodshot blue eyes.

He's lost so much weight that I hardly recognize him. His hair, once kept close to his head, has grown out. Even his voice has changed, now lower and hollow.

He lifts Julia's drink with two fingers and sips out of it.

Julia materializes from nowhere, sees him in her seat, and looks at me like, *what the hell?*

"Julia," I say, "this is an old friend of mine. Julia, James. James, Julia."

"Old friends," he says. "Way back."

"It's a pleasure," she says, but she clutches her purse a little tighter like she knows something's wrong.

"We were just about to leave," I say.

"Good." He checks his watch. "I hate this bar," he says as he turns Julia's drink over on the counter. "Shitty service."

The bartender rushes over, her face tense like she's about to snap, and yells over the counter, "Did you really just dump that out on the fucking table?"

James leans in, his face almost touching hers, and rasps, "No. I spilled it." His words drag across her face.

She snaps her fingers.

"Follow me," James says before a bouncer grabs his arm and drags him out. Julia and I follow them into the alley where the bouncer has already thrown James into a wall.

"I've got him," I say to the bouncer. Julia smiles at him, innocent and ageless. Although I'm not as muscular, I'm bigger than he is.

"Don't let me see any of you in here again," he says before leaving us in the alley.

James steadies himself against the wall as he stands up. "Brody," he coughs and pops a cigarette into his mouth. "I've felt really bad about what happened," he says as he flicks his lighter. "You know, between us." He takes a deep drag and in one motion pockets his lighter and produces a tiny strip of colored dots. "I'd like you to consider this my apology."

"Wait, what is this?" I ask.

Julia leans in and says, "It's acid."

"Smart lady," he grins. "Lysergic acid diethylamide. That's the real shit, too. Fire Acid. That's enough to get very... high." He checks his watch.

"Do you maybe want to go someplace else?" I ask.

James looks around nervously and shrugs.

"We're going to go find another bar." I grab Julia's arm gently and start down the alley.

"You look like you're doing alright," he calls out. "I'm glad. I mean that."

I walk Julia to the sidewalk and backtrack to James. "Hey, I don't know what this is about, but I don't want shit from you." I try to hand him the acid, but he doesn't move.

"That's real, Brody. Keep it. I'm sorry, man, I really am. I've made a lot of mistakes. Just let me fix this one. Okay?"

"I don't know what to say." I pocket the acid.

"You never do." He laughs.

"Fine. Whatever. I'll see you around."

"That's unlikely," he says before he snuffs out his cigarette.

I grab Julia's arm and I walk her down the street until we duck into a dimly-lit club. I pay the cover and excuse myself to go to the bathroom to do a line of coke off the tank of a toilet. I consider calling Tiffany to tell her about seeing James. Instead, I do another line. Then I call.

She has to understand.

I plan to hang up by the fourth ring, but she picks up immediately.

"Hey," Tiffany chimes.

I choke before answering. "Hey, this is Brody."

"I know that. Where are you? Why is there so much noise?"

"Oh, I'm in a bathroom."

Tiff pauses. "Okay."

"How are you?"

"Better."

"Because I'm gone or just better?" I ask.

"This is why I don't answer the phone."

"Well why did you then?"

"I thought I missed you before I heard your voice again. I thought maybe you actually had something to say. Have fun in the bathroom, Broderick." She hangs up on me, so I punch the brick bathroom wall and snort two more lines of coke.

Julia's on the dance floor, so I order a shot of whiskey and down it. Then I order another one and find a booth. Julia finds me when the song ends.

"Are you okay?" When I don't respond she asks, "What are you mad about?"

"Forget it," I say. Her smile fades, and we sit across from each other, music pulsing, strobe lights flashing.

"Do you want a drink?"

She nods.

I go to the bar and order. When I turn around, a Buick of a man is standing at the end of the booth talking to Julia. He leans toward her, his muscles ballooning through his shirt, and Julia laughs at something he said.

I can't help but think about Wayne. In Tiffany's driveway, when I beat on his window and called him out, things could have gone so much worse. He could have stood up for Tiffany. I think about Brian, who seemed so sensible. Yeates who meant to watch us explode. I remember watching Mark dance with Tiffany at the fucking winter ball.

I walk back to the booth and say, "Let's go."

"Can't you see we're having a conversation?" the man asks. "Mind yourself."

"I'm leaving," I say.

"Brody," Julia says, "calm down."

"You need to stop upsetting the lady," the man says, shifting his posture to face me. I punch him in the face. He stumbles back, but I hit him again before he swings at me. He throws his arm too wide, so I duck it easily before I back him into a wall and repeatedly slam my fist into his face and throat.

He collapses against the ground. Something grabs my trembling hands, and I turn, full of violence, to see Julia pulling me toward the door. We turn into the first alley, running into a residential neighborhood.

"What the fuck?" she asks, and I'm so charged, so raw, every nerve ending exposed, that I start to cry. I ball my fists and kneel to the ground, shaking, on the verge of hyperventilating. Julia wraps herself around me, and whispers, "You're okay." She hugs me tighter. "It's going to be okay."

SEVENTY

I'm asleep in my dorm when my phone rings in sharp, incessant bursts.

"Hello," I answer, my voice still full with the gravel of sleep.

"Brody?"

"Yeah?"

"Dude, it's Nolan. Were you asleep? It's like five in the afternoon."

I sigh.

"Anyway, I just thought you should know that James, from high school, um, he died."

"Who?"

"James Schultz. You were friends with him, right?"

"How?"

"Somebody shot him last week in an alley on Bardstown Road. The police think it was gang-related."

"When exactly?" I ask. But I know the answer.

"Last Friday. Doesn't get any more specific."

I dig my student handbook out of my desk drawer and flip through the pages until I find the row of acid drops standing firmly in its disguise as a bookmark. "That sucks. I haven't talked to him since high school."

"I just thought you might want to know."

"I do, man. Thanks for calling." I hang up and get in the shower, turning the heat on full blast. I spent months trying to understand why James set me up for Saul, but I'll never really know why. If he was worried in the alley, then his glassy eyes and devil's smile didn't clue me in. He was always nervous and twitchy, but the truth is I couldn't read him at all.

When I get out of the shower the strip of acid stares at me from my desk.

I pull my jeans on and sit at the foot of my bed, acid in hand, thinking about the night Valerie died. I called James as soon as I got off the phone with her mom and said, "Valerie killed herself." I asked him for hallucinogens at Valerie's funeral to tell her goodbye.

James's father hung himself when James was eight. James came home from school and saw his dad suspended from the ceiling fan.

I guess he understood.

I turn the acid over in my hand and have to admit that I don't know shit about it. James mentioned in high school that people made it with anything from Clorox Bleach to strychnine.

If he were here I'd know the chemical makeup. I'd know the history of LSD in drug culture. How it affected the growth of literature and art.

I pop the tiny, colored tablets off the strip and eat them. Then I lie on the floor and start doing sit ups.

I'm over two hundred when the door swings open and Ken stands in silhouette against the light from the hall. "What's up?" he sings as he throws his backpack in a perfect spiral onto his freshly-made bed.

I stand up all at once.

"Ken. I've never told you this, but... I think it's really cool that you use a backpack."

"Don't fuck with me, Brody. I had a bitch of a day."

"I'm as serious as I've ever been about anything in my entire life." I lift the bag off his bed and stroke the texture. "North. Face." I read the brand out loud, then stare directly into his soul and ask, "What does that even mean?"

"I don't know, man. Probably nothing."

"How can they say it if it doesn't mean anything?" I fall back against my bed and it catches me.

"I don't know," he says as he walks into the bathroom.

"I took some acid."

"You're joking?" he asks, his voice echoing from inside the bathroom. "That shit has, like, drain cleaner and arsenic in it. It stays in your spinal fluid forever."

"Don't worry, Ken. It hasn't even kicked in yet."

He walks out. Washes his hands.

I open my laptop and set my music playlist to randomize. Ken sits at the edge of his bed and eyeballs me as a poppy female singer spits flecks of rainbow dust from the speaker. "Why are you eyeballing me? I ask him."

"It has definitely kicked in."

The vines on my blanket crowd in small patches around my feet and pull themselves, inch by inch, into my skin. "Maybe," I say, watching the vines climb up my leg.

"You just said 'I ask him' out loud. You're fucked." The Rolling Stones's "Paint it Black" replaces the pop song. Ken's face twists into a sour expression. "What's wrong, man?" he asks three times in a row before he kills The Stones.

"B.R.B.," I say.

I stand up and leave the room, walk through the lawn party outside my dorm, and cross the street to Tiffany's. I catch someone walking out the back door as I come to it so I grab the door and brush past her before jogging up at least one thousand stairs to Tiff's floor. I knock on her door for like six minutes.

She opens it and I walk into her room.

"What the fuck are you doing?" she asks.

"I don't know," I say. "I have literally no idea."

"Why aren't you wearing any shoes?" She stands defensively at her bed, gripping the post. Her face is made up like she's going out. Her lips glisten.

"James gave me some acid. And I took it."

"Why?"

"We're all just going to die anyway. What does it matter?"

"God, just get out of here."

"Do you still love me?" I ask. I feel my eyes glaze over. "You said you still love me. I need to know."

"Brody, you're really scaring me."

"Just answer me." I stick my hands in my pockets and feel my keys and my pocket knife. The vines are inside me, wrapped around my spine and tight around the base of my skull.

"Brody, please go." Her eyes flicker. Small bursts of light flash and then die in rapid succession.

"Did you ever?"

She starts crying and walks into the hall. I follow her. "I do love you. You're just so fucking compulsive. You never let anything go. And you're acting like a goddamned psycho."

"Be with me," I say, tears welling up.

"How?" she asks. "You make it impossible. And you keep acting like I cheated on you and fucked up our relationship, but you don't even realize how you treat people. You're a psycho. I never know how you're going to react to anything."

I feel myself crying and I can't stop it.

"You're the only person who knows who I was before this," I say.

"Please, just go."

An ambulance siren blares in the distance. I pull my knife from my pocket and flip out the large blade.

"Brody, stop."

"You're the only person who even knows who she was," I say.

"Someone is going to call the police." She looks behind me. I turn and see two girls at the end of the hall staring at us.

"Good," I say and stab the blade deep into my thigh.

Tiffany erupts in tears, clawing the knife out of my hands as she screams, "Why are you like this!?"

My gaze burrows through her skull where I see one of the girls yelling into her cell. I look back at Tiffany, still crying, then turn around and leave. I slam the hall door and limp down the stairs and back across the street, blood leaking down my leg.

As I stand waiting for the elevator to my dorm, two guys at my right pass each other looks and one of them points to my leg. I look down and see that blood has soaked through my pants.

I really liked these jeans.

Ken is on the phone when I walk back into my room.

"He just walked in. I'll let you know," he says and hangs up. He looks at me, then to my leg. "God, dude." He frantically collects random things from around the room and stuffs them in a bag. "Get anything you need, man. We're leaving this depressing-ass room."

I follow him down the stairs. "Tiff told me what happened. I want to be out of there in case cops come looking for you."

I stop in the hall and touch his shoulder. "You're a good friend, Ken."

"Yeah, shit, I know," he says and pulls me farther down the stairs. We walk through the side door and briskly through the parking lot. Clouds of black smoke burst into existence with every step he takes, then dissipate as quickly as they were born. The smell of pot overwhelms me as I sit in his car. He hands me a towel from his bag and says, "Wrap this around your leg."

He drives us to a hotel. "You can afford this," he says. "I can't."

I slap my wallet on the hotel counter and say, "One room, please."

"How much did you take?" Ken asks as we walk into the hotel room. He sets his bag down and pulls out a first aid kit.

"They were just little dots."

"Take your pants off. I need to see that cut."

I peel the blood-soaked jeans from my leg and start to sit down, but he stops me to lay a towel out on the bed. Then he points at the pants and says, "Just throw those away."

He looks at my legs and sighs. "I knew you were a masochist, but God, man. You need help." He wipes the blood from around the stab wound, but it keeps oozing out. "You need like, real mental help." He pours vodka on my leg and presses harder. "What's being on acid like?"

"It's, like. I can't explain it. It's like seeing colors that you didn't know about. Have you ever heard sound bend?"

"So," Ken asks, "is my face melting off my skull? Are you, like, looking at Ghost Rider?" His eyes pulse with earthly light and I stare, transfixed, into them and watch his irises expand around his corneas.

"Nope." I shake my head to make sure he believes me.

He stitches the cut with a sewing needle and thread. An ambulance blazes somewhere in the distance.

"Where is that fucking siren coming from?" I ask.
He squints. "What siren?"

ONE HUNDRED THOUSAND

Ken goes through three pots of hotel coffee before the sun comes up, then he drives us back to campus because he has a class.

"Can you hang out by yourself for one hour?" His words bend around his mouth.

"Yes."

"Promise?"

"Yes." I simulate an explosion with my fingertips.

I walk with him through the parking lot into the quad. Everything seems to be coming or going, wearing a universe of colors. Reds and browns and yellows bounce past me. A guys walks by in a tie-dye shirt and I understand how colors are made, how they will themselves into existence in my eyes.

Every effect I've ever seen in movies or on screen savers, tie-dyed shirts or hippie vans, is a watery simulation of my new kaleidoscope brain.

In the middle of the courtyard I find an aged tree with limbs that mushroom out to touch the stars. This tree sits in the center of the universe. Yggdrasil. I follow its branches upward and look into the sky. Galaxies of color burst and evaporate.

"Brody!"

I hear the voice in circles. From my seated position at the base of the tree I look for the voice and find Davis holding his hand at face level. "Slap me some skin, homedawg." Davis offers his hand. I slap it, offering him the sacred skin he so deserves. "What's up? How's life?"

"Life is wonderful." I lean against the base of the tree as Davis's eyes train on me, following their target, waiting for a kill shot. They must not find anything because they suddenly change.

They smile.

"I don't know what you're on, but it looks fun. See you around, man." He pats my shoulder and I realize he'd probably light me on fire if it served him. I smile back at him and he disappears into the movement of bodies and colored shirts.

The tree is safe from the movement; under the branches I watch everything. In the corner of my eye I see something moving toward me, fast and uncontrolled. I jerk my head to see it before impact and find that it is replaced by nothing. I reach out and clasp it in my hands.

An old cowboy walks by on his way to a saloon. His stomping fills the sky with flat clouds of deep, matte purple. He stops near me, looks into my soul to read my DNA like binary code. He studies me as I study him until I realize he's made out of cardboard. Then he leaves, rejoining the movement, and the stain of his purple aura dissolves with him.

I lean against the tree and watch time unfold until Ken emerges.

"Salutations, dear friend," I say.

He sighs, offering his hand to me, and says, "Come on, man, let's get breakfast."

We meet Cynthia at the cafeteria. I fill my plate tall with sausage patties, doing my best to feel calm. "How nonchalant am I right now?" I ask Ken.

"Pretty chalant, man. Just try not to think about it."

At the register the cashier looks up at me, her face

twisted in some kind of confusion. She looks to a cashier at another register and says, "Well I'll say it: did you get enough sausage?"

I look at my plate. Then to her. Then to my plate. Then to her. I realize the tragedy of her sausage-hating life. She wastes her days watching students haplessly eat sausage, unaware of her plight. Working so early in the morning, watching a generation of young people who will succeed her. We will build robots to replace her. And the robots will watch us eat sausage.

I look into her tired, wrinkled eyes, say "Fuck you," and hand her my student debit card.

At the table Cynthia and Ken stare tiredly at each other.

"I saw you sitting under your tree," Cynthia says with a giggle as I sit down. She doesn't understand that the tree does not belong to me, but I to it. "Do you think you can get more acid?"

"My supplier is dead."

"Um," she says, "never mind."

I eat one half of one sausage and empty the rest into the garbage. Then I throw the plate and fork away.

Ken and I walk back to the dorm. Ken pats my shoulder as he hails the elevator and the button explodes with sinister, yellow light.

"Alright, man, you've gotta sleep." I watch his mouth say, "I've gotta sleep."

The 9 above the elevator spews the same putrid light. The ninth floor is Julia's. I'll go there and explain the colors bursting and fusing. She'll want to know how colors are made.

"Brody," a voice shouts from behind me. I pivot to see my RA, Alex, standing behind the front desk and staring through me. I look away as fast as I can, back to the elevator, now on the fourth floor. I'm too slow. I'm fucked. Ambulance sirens blare from somewhere inside the building.

"Brody. Come here," he says. Ken looks at me. He knows I'm fucked.

"Package," Alex says as he slings a manila envelope across the counter. It bounces off my chest, but Ken catches it. I reach to grab it out of the air and Ken hands it to me, covering my time-lapse. "Gotta work on those reflexes, bro," Alex chides as he fingers his shark tooth necklace. His eyes never leave mine, never blink. I know he knows. "Are you okay, man?" he asks like he doesn't know, luring me in. This is entrapment.

"I AM!" I yell. The words ring in my ears and I know they're wrong. "THANKS," I say to cover. I need a distraction, so I rip the envelope in two with a single, decisive tear. It explodes with a cloud of dust and detritus. Ken and I cough, and a square inch of carpet falls from the package onto the floor.

"Thanks, Alex," I cough. "I've been waiting for that carpet."

I look at the square inch carpet sample lying on the floor. Ken bends down and snatches it up.

"Dude," Alex says. His steel jaw clenches and his brow furrows. "Seriously, Brody, are you okay?

"He's just tired, man," Ken saves. "Long night." The elevator doors open and I step in, turn on one foot, and salute Alex. He's saying something as the doors shut.

"Does he know?" I ask Ken.

"No, man. Relax."

"I have no fucking clue where that carpet came from," I say.

"I ordered it," he says. "I could only get one sample so I used your name to get another one. I'm going to use them to make a backsplash for the sink."

"Ken," I say, "thank you."

"It's nothing," he says. "Seriously."

"The sirens stopped."

"Good," he says, rubbing his thumb against his new carpet.

SEVENTY-TWO

Ken gets off on our floor and I ride the elevator to the ninth floor and knock on Julia's door until she answers, half-dressed, and motions for me to sit on her bed.

"You know that guy we met last week?" I ask.

She nods.

"Somebody killed him."

She sits down next to me and hugs my shoulders.

"So I took the acid."

She lifts my chin up to look into my eyes. "How much of it?"

"All of it."

"Brody, that was enough for five people."

I shrug and say, "I learned where colors come from."

"Brody," she says, looking hurt.

"I've been high for fifteen hours," I say.

"Brody," she says again, sadder this time. "Brody, why are you crying?"

I look around and realize that this is the first time I've actually been in her room. It's the same as mine but covered in pictures and filled with plush pillows and carpet.

"I'm going to take care of you," she says. "Lie down. You'll feel better if you get some sleep." She lies down and pulls me down next to her. We lie together, my arm draped over her shoulder, and I start sobbing uncontrollably.

"What's wrong?" she mothers.

"I don't know. Nothing." I sit up, willing myself to stop crying. She kneels next to me and strokes my face. "I can't stop."

"Come on, let's get outside." She takes my hand and we wait through the elevator procession again.

"I thought you were tired," Alex says in the lobby.

I stop and watch the muscles twitch in his face.

Julia tugs my arm and leads me outside into the courtyard where we stop at her bench and sit down. She puts her head on my shoulder and holds my chest.

"Why do you always sit out here?" I ask. The sun is baking the skin on my face. White balls of fiber squirm inside my eyes.

"I just like to sit here every once in a while and breathe. You know, appreciate life."

I look at her, deep into her eyes, and start to bawl again.

"Come on," she says and leads me to my car. She opens the passenger side door for me and I climb in before we drive off campus through the mountains. We pass a bridge and stop on the other side of a lake.

On the rock shore of the lake I plant my feet in the murky water. "What is it when you can't stand the thought of living without someone, but you can't stand the thought of ever seeing her again?" I ask, my tears streaming quietly down the sides of my face.

"That's being human," she answers.

That's so easy to say. Everything a person does is human. But I find, as the words digest, there's some comfort in knowing that I'm not so far removed from humanity.

I stand up and walk knee deep into the water. "I should have helped James."

"How?" she asks, still sitting on the shore.

I walk farther into the lake until I'm waist deep.

"Brody." Tears well up in her eyes. "What are you doing?"

Rocks drag against my feet as I plod through the water, now shoulder deep.

"How far do you think it is to the bottom?"

"Get out of the water!" she yells.

I dive into the lake and swim toward the bottom until I can't hold my breath. When I resurface, Julia is rushing toward me.

I dive again.

I swim deeper this time, hold my breath longer.

In the water, as deep as I can swim, I open my eyes and look for the monster. I look deep into the black water and push forward. I open my mouth to let the water in.

Julia grabs the waist of my jeans and pulls, kicking wildly toward shore.

There's something desperate about her rescue attempt. Heartbreaking. She couldn't pull me out of the water if her life depended on it.

But she's trying anyway. She's here and the monster isn't.

We swim to shore and she clamps herself to me, our bodies slick, and I feel her heart beat violently against my chest.

"I should have helped Valerie, too," I say, staring directly into the noon sun to avoid looking at Julia's reaction. "I might as well have killed her myself."

"What are you talking about?" I can hear the tears in her quivering voice.

I can't bring myself to explain. I struggle to remember Valerie's voice, her laugh, but I can't.

When I don't respond, Julia threads her fingers through mine and says, "I was eight years old when I first thought about killing myself. We lived in this huge house, like three stories. And then my dad left. I climbed up on the roof, and I sat there just thinking about how easy it would be. But I didn't, and things worked out okay. People make choices, Brody. I don't know what happened, but whatever it was it wasn't your fault."

She holds me until our clothes dry.

"I think I'm ready to get some sleep," I say.

We get in the car. She rolls the windows down as we start across the bridge.

"Who's Valerie?" she asks.

"A girl I used to love," I say. "She's dead."

Julia strokes the side of my face. "Tell me about her."

And I do.

EPILOGUE

I wake up next to Julia in a familiar hotel room. She's naked, looking more peaceful than she ever does awake. I rise gently, trying not to rouse her, but her arm darts up and she caresses my face gently before turning over and drifting away.

I pull the shades open to the pale, lavender-gray of dawn.

I take a very long shower, still feeling the creeping pull of the acid. When I get out, I lean against the sink and inspect my face in the mirror. My eyes are bloodshot over dark, sickly circles.

I leave the bathroom and root around for any remnants of liquor or cocaine. The sun peeks over the tree line and I lean against the window watching it rise.

Julia stirs, her naked body beautiful and inviting.

"Close the blinds," she croaks and rolls over.

I consider closing them, and then I realize that even in the morning hours with the sun hailing a new start and a beautiful, naked girl lying in bed waiting for my return, I can't stand being who I am.

I get dressed quickly and settle the hotel bill before I go to my dorm room and pack. Ken is asleep with his textbooks strewn around him on the floor.

I stuff my clothes and computer into my bag, leaving everything else; there's no sense in taking any of it. I consider waking Ken up to tell him I'm going, but I feel guilty enough and can't bring myself to do it, so I stand in the doorway thinking that I should at least say something. Then someone walks by and I realize I'm watching Ken sleep, so I feel like a creep and close the door as quietly as possible.

On my way home my phone vibrates in my pocket. I turn the radio off and answer.

"Hey, where are you?" Julia asks.

"Gone," I say.

"Do you feel any better?" she asks.

"Look, um, hey." I get the sense she knows something is wrong, especially after I left her at the hotel, but she stays silent so I continue. "I'm not in town. I'm going home." She doesn't say anything, forcing me to continue. "I'm not coming back."

"You left me and you didn't even tell me?" Her crying is muffled, strained, her furtive nature betrayed by a simple moment of honesty.

I fight the urge to console her, to thank her, to tell her that I love her or that things will be alright. Instead, I remind her, "I'm not coming back."

I wait for a moment, listening to her cry, before I hang up.

I scroll through my phone book and consider calling her back. Maybe calling Tiffany. Maybe even Ken. Instead, I delete every number from my phone. Then I call the phone company to change my number.

Afterward, I roll all of the windows down and throw the phone out. It bounces on the pavement twice before it shatters.

The blue sky seems tangible, like I could reach out and touch it.

With my arm hanging out the window, I take a long, deliberate breath, taking great pleasure in the sweet, Kentucky air.

Made in the USA
Middletown, DE
19 January 2021